GAGNON
HOME

JACQUARD
FARM

MILES

NORMANDY
INVASION

WE WERE THERE
AT THE
NORMANDY INVASION

"The 82nd always wins its battles!" Slim said

WE WERE THERE
AT THE
NORMANDY
INVASION

Written and Illustrated by
CLAYTON KNIGHT

Historical Consultant:
MAJOR GENERAL RALPH ROYCE
U.S.A.F., RETIRED

GROSSET & DUNLAP
PUBLISHERS, NEW YORK

PRINTED IN THE UNITED STATES OF AMERICA
LIBRARY OF CONGRESS CATALOG CARD NO. 56-5389

We Were There at the Normandy Invasion

Contents

[*v*]

CONTENTS

Illustrations

WE WERE THERE
AT THE
NORMANDY INVASION

CHAPTER ONE

Dangerous Business

TOWARD sunset on the first day of June, a small black car rattled past a crossroads sign in a tiny village in northwestern France. The sign pointed to the near-by town of Sainte Mère Église, about two miles farther inland. The coast of the English Channel was nearly three miles back in the other direction.

Behind the wheel of the car sat a thin, anxious Frenchman. Hunched beside him was a young, blond Englishman. The younger man was shabbily dressed, and most of the lower part of his face was covered by a bandage.

The car pulled up and stopped in front of a house with a weather-beaten sign on it which read:

PIERRE GAGNON *Gas Tobacco Chocolate*

A lone gas pump stood between the house and the highway. Beyond the house lay Pierre Gagnon's farm.

The driver waited a moment and then honked three times sharply. Almost immediately the door opened. A dark-haired boy of about twelve came out.

The man behind the wheel asked, "Is your father here?"

The boy nodded and politely explained, "If you want gas I can work the pump."

The driver frowned nervously and repeated, "Get your father."

From the direction of Ste. Mère Église three German soldiers came in sight, their heavy tread echoing in the stillness of the drowsy village. Both men in the car and the boy glanced at them. When the boy did not move, the driver spoke more sharply, "Your father, bring him here."

The boy turned and disappeared through the door.

The driver and his passenger waited. The younger man slid low in his seat, his back toward the approaching soldiers.

Chatting among themselves, the Germans paid no attention to the car nor to a girl of fifteen who had come to the house door. Behind her stood her father, Pierre Gagnon, a burly man with a thick mustache, and rumpled country clothes.

He brushed past the girl, and at a signal from the driver, went to the pump. The driver left his seat and bent close to speak to him.

At a signal from the driver he went to the pump

Pierre Gagnon listened carefully, then swung around and went back to the girl in the doorway.

"Marie," he whispered, "they want us to hide this fellow, another downed flyer, for two or three days."

The girl studied the youth slumped low in the front seat. She thought, "He looks like all the airmen who are shot down over France—the worried eyes, the peasant clothes that don't fit, the bandages."

"Who is the driver?" she asked. "Has he the right password?"

"Yes," her father replied. "And he asks us to hide this English pilot till the Maquis can find a way to get him over the border into Spain. Do you think we can do it?"

In Normandy, that part of France which thrusts northward into the English Channel, apple trees were in bloom. Warm, soft breezes played across the green fields, over the thick hedgerows, and through the orchards.

But in this beautiful spring of 1944 the people of Normandy could not enjoy what they saw. They could only hear the tramp of German boots over their land. Nazi armies had occupied France, and for the last two years German camps had been set up over the countryside. French property had been seized, and Nazi officers told the people exactly what they could and could not do.

The town of Ste. Mère Église sits almost in the middle of what is called the Cherbourg Peninsula. Most of the Norman people are farmers or dairymen. Some are fishermen, but the Nazis would not let them fish. Instead, the Germans set up barriers along the shore to prevent boats from landing. And they lined the coast with huge guns. Also, the fields were spiked with posts and barbed wire to keep American and British gliders from landing.

For many months, the French people had been expecting British and American armies to come in a great invasion that would drive the Nazis out. But their hopes had always failed. No troops had come to liberate them, and the Normans felt glum and often angry. More than anything else they wanted to be free.

The only thing they could do was to cause all possible trouble for the Nazis secretly. Those who banded together in "Underground" or Resistance groups were called Maquis. If a Maquis was caught by the Germans he was very likely to be shot.

Nevertheless, many French ran the risk of being detected helping the British and Americans. Even very young men and girls operated in the secret Underground.

The Nazis tried to watch everyone, but sometimes the most innocent-looking car on the road was being used to trick them, even in the quietest village.

It was happening now. Marie Gagnon nodded to her father. "Bring him in," she whispered. "I'll get the room in the attic ready."

"One moment," her father said. "I'll send André out of the way first. What he doesn't know he won't chatter about."

He shouted through the door, "André. Come here."

There was a clatter of heavy shoes and the boy reappeared.

"Son," his father said sternly, "have you taken the eggs to old Schmidt yet?"

André hesitated and shook his head. "No—my bicycle—I could not get the chain fixed."

His sister snorted at him. "You are getting soft. It won't hurt you to walk. The eggs are on the kitchen table."

André thought, "Sisters!" But a look at his father's face sent him back for the eggs.

As he turned down the road toward Ste. Mère Église his father went back to the gas pump. André had not gone far when Patchou, his dog, caught up with him. The puppy gave him a playful nudge as if to say, "I'm sorry to be late, but I had to give that car a good, long sniff."

After walking less than a mile, André turned off and came to a group of camouflaged barracks. Inside the high wire fence, narrow buildings stood in long rows. A German sentry, his rifle held loosely, guarded the gate. He grinned at the boy and waved him inside.

As André entered, a Frenchman pedaling by on an ancient bicycle shouted to him, but a burst of Patchou's barking drowned out the greeting.

André went around a large group of military vehicles and mobile guns parked under a protecting netted screen. Then he followed a winding path up to one of the barracks.

Patchou, prancing ahead of him, leaped playfully at a middle-aged German soldier seated on a bench outside, puffing on his pipe.

Gently pushing off the excited dog, the German saw André and called, "Aha! It's young Herr Gagnon." He tapped the ashes from his pipe and then added, "You have brought Papa Schmidt some more eggs, no?"

André held out the package. The German placed it on the bench and carefully unknotted the big handkerchief the boy had brought.

Schmidt exclaimed when he saw the contents. "*Ach!* and cheese, too." He held the cheese to his nose and inhaled deeply. "That's goot. You are a fine boy, André Gagnon." With a twinkling smile, he added, "Almost as goot as my own Otto.

"Look, I show you." He reached into the pocket of his tunic. "Just today a letter came from my home in Osnabrück—and pictures." Pointing to one, he said, "That's my Otto. He's like you, no?"

André studied the snapshot of a boy about his own age but with light, almost white hair, frowning into the sun.

A little embarrassed, André could only say, "He wears funny clothes."

The German chuckled. "If he could see you, he'd think yours were comical too."

Glancing at the letter in his hand, he sighed. "*Ach!* but they are having it bad in Osnabrück. The Englisher and the Americaner planes they bomb, bomb, bomb our town. Part of my home is gone. My wife and boy say they get no sleep."

Almost to himself he muttered, "When will the war end?" Then, turning to the boy, he said sadly, "*Ach,* how do you know, any more than me? We smile, eh, while we can . . . and enjoy the sunshine."

Patchou had wandered off to one of the other barracks and started a fight with one of the camp dogs. André called over his shoulder, "I'll be back again in a day or two," and ran to separate the two animals.

By the time he and Patchou reached home, the last twilight had faded. The house was dark, for blackout curtains were drawn across the windows.

Inside, his sister sat hunched alone in the wide, stone-floored kitchen, listening to music from a forbidden radio.

"Where's Papa?" André asked.

Marie looked annoyed. "He's gone off with Victor Lescot. That Raoul Cotein is making trouble again. Now he says our cows broke into his pasture. What an old weasel he is! Even the Germans behave better."

Later, with supper over, she paused suddenly, and raised her hand for André to be silent.

Breaking the stillness, the weird wail of air-raid sirens rose far away.

Marie looked tired. And there was fear in her eyes when she heard the sirens, which meant that another air raid was beginning.

"*Again* tonight," she sighed, "and so early. It is not yet ten o'clock."

She went to the kitchen window and made sure the black curtains let no light through.

"You run upstairs, André, and see that the curtains there are tight. And stay with Mother," she ordered.

Mme. Gagnon had been ill for several weeks. Now she lay in her big bed upstairs, nearly asleep.

She opened her eyes as the sirens died away and then began again.

"Well, son," she said, "did you eat a good supper?"

André nodded.

A little wind from the sea had sprung up, and somewhere a loose board rattled. Also, there was a noise in the attic. "Must be a rat," André said to himself, and decided to take Patchou up there tomorrow. "He'll have some fun catching that little thief," he thought.

His mother was roused again by the drone of plane engines coming in high overhead. Their lofty beating made the air tremble. Antiaircraft guns in near-by Ste. Mère Église began to boom. Their hollow *wumpf, wumpf,* added to the din of the sirens.

In a slight lull, Mme. Gagnon asked, "Is your father home? I do not like him to be away when there is an air raid."

André shook his head and raised his voice above the racket. "He's out with Victor. Marie says Raoul Cotein is trying to stir up trouble again."

He wanted his mother to think of something other than the air raid, so he laughed and added, "Marie says Raoul is a weasel."

Raoul Cotein's mischief-making was a village joke.

Mme. Gagnon sighed. "I wish your father would come home," she said. "The bombing might be bad."

"Don't worry," André said wisely. "These are

English planes. The Americans only come in the daytime. You know, Maman, there aren't any big guns and bridges and war factories close to us here."

But bombs were dropping, though at a distance. Several minutes later, the coastal guns were still firing, but the sound of the engines had begun to die away.

"Listen," said Mme. Gagnon in a relieved voice. "You were right, André, they dropped no bombs on us."

André heard his sister's footsteps on the stairs. Then he thought he heard the creak of the attic door. Presently she came bustling into the room, carrying a small tray with a pot of chocolate and a cup.

Cheerfully, she said, "There, Maman, they've gone. Let's hope we get no more planes tonight. Here," pouring the chocolate, "drink this and try to get back to sleep."

Her dark skirts swished around her knees as she fluffed up her mother's pillows and tucked in the coverlet.

Downstairs the front door opened and they heard Pierre Gagnon calling, "Marie!"

Then someone spoke in another voice.

"Shh-h," whispered Marie. "There is someone with Papa."

Her father was saying loudly, "Yes, Herr Kapitan, I'm all right. No, no, it is not necessary for you to come in."

Before Marie and André reached the head of the stairs, the outside door was slammed, bolted, and the stranger had gone.

The light from the hall lamp fell on their father as he turned to face the stairs.

Across one of his cheeks stretched a deep red gash.

CHAPTER TWO

House-to-House Search

A<small>S</small> THE light fell across the wound on her father's face Marie cried out sharply.

From the bedroom Mme. Gagnon called, "Marie, what's wrong?"

André ran back to her side. "Papa's hurt," he said, and then added hastily, "but not badly."

"But there were no bombs," Mme. Gagnon exclaimed.

Pierre himself had lunged up the stairs and now burst into the bedroom sputtering, "Don't excite yourself, Maman. All is well. No harm is done. That *cochon!*"

"Ah," his wife cried. "So, it *was* Raoul Cotein!"

"Who else but that son of Satan?" Gagnon's eyes snapped fiercely. He was red and breathing furiously, and flung himself into a chair beside the bed.

"I contain myself," he said firmly, clamping both great hands on his knees like thunderclaps.

"No, Papa," André grasped his arm, "do not contain yourself yet. Tell us what has happened."

"Marie," said Mme. Gagnon, "run get some hot water and clean Papa's cut."

Marie clattered quickly down the stairs and Mme. Gagnon went on, "Now, Pierre, you get yourself slashed and perhaps poisoned over a cow. I thought you had more sense."

The farmer stiffened. "It was *not* about a cow! Raoul sent for me only as an excuse. Ask Victor. He also was there. At once Raoul began to scream so loud, if it were not for the guns booming they could have heard him in Ste. Mère."

"Then what—?" began Mme. Gagnon impatiently.

"Then," cried Pierre, "he began to shout charges against me." He swept out both arms. "Against all of us."

Pierre swallowed angrily. "He accused me," he said, "of being a collaborator of the Nazis! He accuses us all—you, Marie, André—of working hand in glove with them. It seems that only this evening he saw André, here, entering the German camp."

There it was—the black word, *collaborator*, he who helps the enemy! It meant someone hated by all Frenchmen, more, perhaps, than the enemy.

"But Papa," André cried angrily, "poor old Schmidt! He is not an enemy."

Pierre shook his head. "He is. We have only been giving him a few eggs and a little cheese because he is a tired old man. But Raoul can make it sound wrong if he wants to."

Mme. Gagnon nodded encouragement. She thought of the many Allied flyers this brave, shaggy man had secretly helped to escape from the Nazis at the risk of his life. And of the boy in the attic. She glanced at her son, who, so far, knew nothing about his father's and sister's work in the Underground.

"I grew very angry when he called me a collaborator," Pierre went on. "How could I let anyone say such a thing to me? I punched Raoul and he came back at me like a bull. We fell down, and my face struck the stone wall. The result is not pretty, perhaps?"

"Why did that German captain come home with you?" André burst out. "Did he get in the fight with Raoul?"

Gagnon snorted. "Not in the fight. Unfortunately he came along just as Raoul picked up a stick and started for me. Victor was yelling at both of us, and suddenly we saw the German coming. Naturally we all shut our mouths like clams. Frenchmen do not fight Frenchmen in front of the Nazis—not even Raoul."

"Perhaps there will be no more to it," said Mme. Gagnon soothingly.

"If they do not send soldiers to snoop around the house," Pierre grunted, "we need not worry."

Marie returned, breathless, with a basin of water and clean cloths. Her father sat on the edge of the bed, repeating the story, while the cut was cleaned and gently covered with ointment.

"Your face feels better, Pierre?" Mme. Gagnon asked. "Good. Now we must all sleep."

A few minutes later the house was dark. Everywhere, from the kitchen where André snuggled into his goosedown-soft, curtained bed, to the attic, there was the sound of quiet breathing. And in the attic the English boy turned restlessly on his narrow cot.

Before dawn the household roused to the day's

duties. It was not long before they heard news. The weary, older German soldiers were being removed. War-toughened young Nazis were going to take over the district.

Before the new troops had been in camp two days, proclamations that put stricter limits on freedom were posted everywhere.

A curfew was ordered. People must not leave their houses between ten in the evening and five in the morning. This did not bother André since he usually went to bed well before ten.

A sad little good-by note from Papa Schmidt reached him. It thanked the family warmly for their kindness and ended: "Be a goot boy. Someday I bring my Otto to see you. *Auf Wiederzehen.*"

André noticed that the German camp was a changed place. The new regiment had chained vicious police dogs inside the wire fence. And André was horrified when he heard that stray dogs belonging to the village people had been shot.

He tied Patchou safely in the farmyard at the rear of the house, and kept an eye on him.

Then came another dreaded order:

ALL ARTICLES OF BRASS OR COPPER MUST BE SURRENDERED BY THE CIVILIAN POPULATION. A HOUSE-TO-HOUSE SEARCH WILL BE MADE.

André's most prized possession was a gleaming brass trumpet which he had learned to play with some skill. It was not only dear to him, but the only really precious thing he owned. "I must hide it in some very, very safe place," he thought.

Also, the coming search would be very dangerous to the rest of the family. If the Germans came they would surely find the flyer in their attic. And if an enemy pilot were found in their house they would all be shot.

Marie and her father had been watching for the Maquis operator to come for the flyer, according to plan. But for some reason he had not yet appeared.

"Those Maquis! They are wasting their time in some café, enjoying themselves, probably," Mme. Gagnon said irritably.

But Pierre replied, "No. Not the Maquis. There is some good reason why the operator has not yet been able to get here."

It was not until June 4th, just before curfew time, that a Maquis messenger slipped into the Gagnon house.

He said he could not come before because the new Nazi garrison had sent patrols everywhere.

The plans of the Underground had all been changed. Pierre and Marie, he said, must keep the flyer where he was until new arrangements to spirit him away could be made.

That evening Marie and her father huddled in the dark little parlor to talk over their situation.

Marie whispered wildly, "What *shall* we do if the Nazis come here? They will go to the attic too."

Pierre shrugged, scowling. "We must find some way. We always have before."

But, more than an hour later, they still had no idea what to do.

"There's no other way," whispered M. Gagnon at last, "but to go ask Father Duprey to offer some idea. He must be taken into the secret."

Marie nodded.

The night was dark and rain began to fall.

Her father yawned. "I'll go see Father Duprey tomorrow, first thing," he said. "Now off to bed with you."

They rose, and stood tensely, startled by a creak on the stairs and soft, padding footsteps outside the door.

The door opened and André stood there, clutching his boots and his trumpet.

"Heavens, André, you frightened us," Marie snapped. "We thought you were in bed long ago."

His father asked gruffly, "Where are you going at this hour?"

The boy moved nervously. "Papa," he blurted, "why didn't you tell me that man was hiding in the attic?"

Pierre and his daughter exchanged quick glances. Pierre put a hand protectingly on his son's shoulder. "We thought it might save trouble if you didn't know," he said. "But now it's done."

"But why shouldn't I know?" André demanded stubbornly. "He's the man with the bandage who came in the car a few days ago, isn't he? I talked to him. And I like him."

"You must be sure not to give us away," André's father ordered sternly. "Say nothing about this man to anyone. Do you understand?"

André promised, and he laid his trumpet beside the lamp. "I found him up there when I went to the attic to get this. I must bury it outside somewhere before the Nazis come snooping around." Then he gasped. "But won't they find Ronald?"

His father said, "Your sister and I are looking out for him. Now, about this trumpet . . . ?"

The horn *had* to be hidden before another morning.

"I'll bury it near the fence beside the lane," André whispered as he edged out into the stormy darkness.

An eerie stillness hung heavy on Marie and her father when André had gone.

After a few moments Marie whispered nervously, "I don't think I can sleep until this is settled, Papa. Don't you think you could slip out and see Father Duprey tonight?"

Pierre frowned. "What about this cursed curfew? I do not want to be caught. However, it will not be my first night job for the Underground."

He slipped on his coat, pulled his cap low, and eased himself noiselessly out of the house.

Marie sat alone, her eyes on the clock.

Her heart jumped a beat when an approaching patrol car whizzed down the road. It passed the house. Again the dark silence.

The back door opened and André returned, his boots caked high with mud. When he asked, "Where's Papa?" she said, "He has gone out. Ask no more questions and go to bed."

"I will wait for Papa," he replied firmly, and perched on the edge of a chair, studying his sister's face.

He had felt excitement growing among the others in the house. Now it belonged to him, too.

They listened for outside noises through the sounds of the storm. André said, "Ronald Pitt's a fighter pilot, Marie. Did you know that?

"I never talked to one before," he continued. "He told me his Spitfire plane got hit, late one evening, and he parachuted down into a wood. The Germans didn't find him. He's been hiding in the fields and towns for two weeks."

Marie nodded. "He's one of the lucky ones— so far."

André chattered softly on. "Those bandages

were a fake, weren't they? He wasn't really hurt. Somebody painted his jaw with iodine and put on those bandages so he wouldn't have to talk to any Germans."

Her eyes on the clock, Marie said, "Shush now."

André broke the next few minutes of silence with, "Ronald comes from Nottingham, like Robin Hood—"

But Marie hissed, "Shh-h!" still more sharply, and rose to listen at the door.

At a rap outside, she unfastened the lock.

Pierre slipped inside. His tired face had lighted up, and Marie smiled. "Father Duprey will help us!" she cried eagerly.

Pierre motioned to the stairs and said, "We go talk to Maman quickly. Come, Marie. You, André, clothes off and into bed. Lamps out, Marie."

At Mme. Gagnon's bedside a candle flickered. Pierre and Marie drew close beside the pillow.

"The Nazis have already begun to search houses on the other road," Pierre whispered rapidly. "They are still a long way from us, but we can't lose any time. Father Duprey has a plan. It is this. He will arrange with the hospital at St. Sauveur le Vicomte tomorrow for you to go there in an ambulance to have treatments. And we will hide the English flyer inside the ambulance."

At a frightened look from Mme. Gagnon, he

went on hurriedly, "Marie will ride with you, and Father Duprey will sit up with the driver. He thinks if we make a big parade of it the Germans will not be so suspicious."

"But St. Sauveur is beyond Ste. Mère Église . . . so far away," whispered Mme. Gagnon.

"But that is good, Maman," Marie protested.

"It is the nut of the whole idea!" Pierre's voice rose excitedly. "St. Sauveur is out of this district, and you will be safely away from these new Nazi troops. Some Maquis will meet us near the hospital. They will spirit our flyer out of the ambulance and hide him until he can be moved on. It is a good plan, Maman?"

"I do not like it," she protested.

CHAPTER THREE

Father Duprey's Plan

Even next morning when Father Duprey arrived to go over the plan again, Mme. Gagnon was still protesting uneasily.

Father Duprey clasped his hands, beaming. "Think of the good that will come to all."

Marie's mother nodded her head doubtfully.

The next step after preparing Mme. Gagnon for her role was to instruct the flyer in his part.

Leaving Marie on watch downstairs, Pierre and the priest, trailed by André, clumped up the dark staircase to the attic.

Ronald Pitt listened to them quietly and shrugged when Father Duprey asked, "You agree, my son? It is a good scheme, you think?"

"Well, I'm in your hands," the young Englishman replied. "But I'd certainly feel foul if I got you into trouble. Of course, I'm willing to take any kind of chance. The sooner I get back to my squadron the better. I think you can guess what's up in England. It's my bet the invasion is coming any day now."

"It can't come too soon," Pierre said eagerly.

Soon after that, work on the farm began as on an ordinary day. In spite of the Gagnons' desire to appear untroubled, however, they paused often to listen and look around them.

Rumors of the Nazi search party reached them from all sides. The village women trundled from house to house bemoaning the loss of their copper cooking pots.

At two o'clock that afternoon the priest's housekeeper brought a package. A message said that all arrangements had been completed. At exactly four o'clock the ambulance would arrive before Pierre's house. Mme. Gagnon was to be ready to leave instantly. The party must arrive at a point near the hospital at *exactly* five o'clock.

Marie packed clothes for her mother and laid out her own best dress. Even though she would be returning that same evening, she also prepared a small lunch basket. The hospital was only about eighteen miles away, but food might be difficult to find and expensive to buy.

André was given the job of coaching Ronald Pitt. He climbed the attic stairs filled with excitement but also full of laughter. For the disguise that Father Duprey had chosen for the flyer was a nun's outfit of clothing.

When the young Englishman had put on the long, full, black robe, André stood back and studied him, his eyes dancing. And from under the starched headdress that framed his narrow face the flyer's blue eyes danced just as gaily.

André said, "You make a pretty nun." And grinning, he finished, "I did not think Spitfire pilots were so *chic.*"

Then recalling the serious instructions his father had given him for Ronald, he repeated them. "Be ready to come downstairs just before four o'clock. Get into the ambulance quickly, right after they put Maman's stretcher in. The family will try to surround you. The driver is a Maquis and he's used to this kind of business.

"Now," André finished, "my father says to be sure you don't leave anything behind you for the Germans to find. And Marie will come in a few minutes to put the cot and all this stuff away."

"Splendid." Ronald looked down at the boy. "I'd hate to see *my* young brother exposed to all this danger you're so cheerful about. Well, now I must practice a bit." He took a sedate turn between the cot and the window, grinning at the French boy. And he practiced sitting down demurely.

It had been raining gustily all day but stopped about three, and the wind dropped.

For some time the village had been quiet—the Nazi squad busy among outlying farms.

As four o'clock neared, Mme. Gagnon was upstairs, dressed and wrapped in a shawl, ready to be hurried onto the stretcher.

In the shuttered little parlor, a dark-robed figure stood in the shadow beside the hallway door.

André stood watch at a window on the road, and his father and Marie paced the stone-floored kitchen.

Then, electrically, the silence was broken by the rumble of an approaching car. André drew the curtain aside a little.

At his stifled cry Marie and her father rushed to the window.

A German army truck crammed with armed soldiers was slowing up on the road. And at that same moment, from the opposite direction, the closed black ambulance rolled up to the Gagnon door.

Almost before the ambulance had braked to a stop Father Duprey's tall, erect figure swung down from the front seat, and Pierre rushed to admit him. The driver immediately began to back the long vehicle close to the door.

Marie cried softly, "Heavens, Father, what a calamity! The Nazis! What can we do?"

"We can act sensible," said Father Duprey, "and waste no time moaning about what we can't help. Those men are evidently going to search the Julliard farm next door before they come here. Let the driver in with the stretcher, daughter, so we lose no time getting Mme. Gagnon away."

The driver sidled in and M. Gagnon seized the stretcher. The two men hurried up the stairs.

A few seconds later the creaking steps warned André that his mother was being carried down. He signaled Ronald to be ready for his dash.

"Now," said Father Duprey to Marie, "sob a little, but not enough to draw much attention."

André held the door while the little procession puffed and brushed through. Mme. Gagnon was lifted easily in through the ambulance door. And a moment later, Ronald, clutching his awkward bundle of skirts as naturally as he could, climbed in and crouched beside the stretcher. His face was hidden by the width of his headdress, and he bent gently over the sick woman.

"It is all going like clockwork, madame," he whispered. "Don't be frightened."

"I—I'm afraid," murmured Mme. Gagnon, "more for Pierre, for Marie and André . . ."

Standing by the road, Pierre looked with mounting anxiety at the soldiers prowling through the farm next door. They were not spending much time there.

In all his later life André never forgot the next few minutes.

Mme. Gagnon called, "Pierre! Pierre, please come with me."

And just then Raoul Cotein bicycled briskly up, shouting, *"Mon Dieu,* Gagnon, what are you up to now?"

He set his bicycle against the wall and stared into the open end of the ambulance.

"What's the trouble here?" he demanded loudly as his eyes rolled toward the strange nun.

"Get on with your business, Raoul," M. Gagnon ordered. "My wife is ill, as you well know, and you are not needed here."

Father Duprey's black eyes were traveling swiftly from the hunched figures in the dimness of the ambulance to the Germans only two or three hundred yards away.

André boosted Marie in beside her mother, and M. Gagnon closed the door upon them. Father Duprey said calmly, "You may as well come along, Pierre. It will comfort your wife. I'll see that you and Marie get home tonight."

"But André—" Pierre whispered.

André tugged at his arm. "Go. Go, Papa," he urged. "I can take care of everything—only go."

Down the road, the Nazis were piling back into their truck and the starter whined.

Father Duprey seized Pierre's arm and whipped

He opened the door to find a Nazi officer frowning at him

him swiftly forward and up to the seat in front.

He had no more than slid into the seat himself when the Maquis driver rocked the old ambulance into action with a crash of gears. The machine swayed into a turn and roared away toward Ste. Mère Église.

André watched it go for a long minute.

The German army truck started, but halted a little distance off, and the sharp voice of the officer giving commands drifted toward them.

Raoul Cotein shifted his feet. "Uh— I have things to do," he cried suddenly. He flung a leg over his bicycle, and peddling furiously, was soon gone.

André moved idly toward the house. Once through his own door, the boy trotted quickly into the kitchen.

He untied his dog and put him in the dimly lit cow barn. As he snapped the door fastening, he spoke warningly, "Not a sound out of you, Patchou. Remember!"

He got back into the house just in time to answer a loud thumping at the front door. He opened it to find a Nazi officer and several hard-faced soldiers frowning down at him.

CHAPTER FOUR

Midnight Landing

ANDRÉ stepped quickly aside as, without a word, the Germans tramped in.

Three of them were ordered upstairs while the others set to work poking into every cupboard and drawer on the first floor. When they had emptied the kitchen of its copper they trooped off to the outbuildings.

André waited uncertainly in the hallway at first. Later, he edged his way to the farmyard door and anxiously watched the search through the barns. Not until he saw that none of the men went toward the lane where his trumpet was buried did he begin to breathe easily.

At last, the officer came from the loft over the cow barn, shouting to his men to return to the truck.

He strode into the kitchen and asked André,

"Your father and mother—where are they?"

"They are all gone to the hospital with my mother, who is sick," André explained.

"Well, then, when your father returns," the officer snapped, "tell him I am putting men with machine guns in that loft overlooking the road. And advise him that it will do no good to protest."

André's heart sank. What would the family do with a lot of Nazis underfoot? Did they suspect that the Gagnons had been working with the Underground?

Now, for the first time, he felt desperately alone. He nodded silently.

When the Germans had gone—with his mother's copper kettles—André ran back to the barn. Patchou lay in his dark corner under a manger, as quiet as a mouse.

"Come into the house, Patchou," he said. "We'll have to keep you there now."

For an hour or so André went about doing his father's chores and his own. The heavy, low-lying clouds began breaking a little.

He had just finished milking the cows when the German truck returned with a dozen rough-looking gunners and the sharp-faced officer. Machine guns were unloaded and hauled up the stone loft steps.

Some time later the officer and some of the men piled into the truck and drove away.

"They must have left at least six up there," André said to himself. He must go up the road later, and warn his father and Marie about the hidden gunners.

He opened the front window so that he might be warned of an approaching car.

André ate the cold supper Marie had left under a cloth for him. The minutes dragged by. By nine

o'clock there had been no sign of his father and sister, and no word. For a while he sat on the floor beside his dog. Tomorrow was June 6th— Patchou's first birthday. André hoped Marie would keep her promise to bring back some sort of toy to celebrate the occasion.

When the clock struck ten he went out into the deepening twilight to stare into the gloom toward Ste. Mère. What if the Nazis had opened the ambulance and found Ronald? Perhaps the Maquis had failed to meet them . . . He tried not to think of such things.

Now it was eleven o'clock and long past time to go to bed. From several directions there was strong antiaircraft firing, and the echo of bombs.

In spite of the curfew order, André began to walk stealthily down the road. Those Nazi gunners might open fire on any vehicle bringing his family home.

Halting, listening, he picked his way to a bend of the highway. After a little while he began to realize how tired he was.

Drowsily he looked for a sheltered spot in the hedge, and sank down among the ferns and the tall grass. The rich smell of earth and spring growth rose around him. A few fields away a horse whinnied, and from far in the distance came the long, high-fluted note of a train whistle. . . .

Some time later he awoke with a start, and wondered where he was and how long he had slept. All around him hung thick, velvety blackness.

Something had wakened him. It was the sirens and fire alarms in Ste. Mère.

And then he heard the planes.

Drumming overhead, throbbing so that the earth shook under his feet, he heard them coming.

Then he saw them. A brilliant moon outlined their wings.

He ran across the road and struggling through a hedge, scrambled quickly up the tallest of a clump of trees.

And now he saw that the planes were coming in from the west, lower than he had ever seen them fly. They were twin-motored, scooping below the clouds to right and left, filling the sky.

They were bombing Normandy! Ste. Mère! Perhaps a bomb would drop on him—NOW!

The din of the German guns was incessant, and the roar of the plane engines was deafening. He must descend and find a ditch. His arms ached, but he could not let go. He had climbed as high as there were limbs to support him, and now he clung to the solid trunk.

He noticed one particular plane coming directly toward him. It was etched sharply against a luminous patch of cloud, and he could clearly see the three white stripes that banded each wing.

As he watched, he saw the open door at the rear of the fuselage, and instantly something dark dropped from it. Then another dark blob and another.

Expecting the whistle of bombs, he shut his eyes, pressed his face into the rough bark, and prayed . . .

After a few seconds he opened his eyes.

Other than the guns and the throttled beat of the engines, there had been no sound. No bombs were exploding.

André threw his head back and glanced quickly skyward. In the moonlight, speckled in every direction across the sky, hung hundreds of mushroom shapes that were floating gently earthward as silently as apple petals.

Suddenly he saw that they were parachutes!

And below nearly every one, a soldier swung. From the lowest he could make out the jut of rifles.

CHAPTER FIVE

André's Warning

CLINGING to his uncertain perch, for the first few seconds André felt stunned. Could this be his own Normandy sky? He watched the flicker of moonlight here and there on the parachutes drifting down through the scudding clouds.

"The Invasion!" he thought.

He had turned to stare across at his father's barn in the distance, wondering about the Nazi machine gunners, when the tree beside him was torn by a crashing of branches. His heart leaped into his throat. The topmost branches were entwined by a great, pale, crumpled parachute. And, dangling from the shroud lines, hung a figure that swung like a pendulum.

In the meadow beyond, other dark shapes were pelting into the hayfield, their chutes collapsing around them like punctured balloons.

The noise was spreading. Isolated shots and short bursts of machine-gun fire drummed, stopped, and drummed again. From the far-off German camp near Ste. Mère came the wail of a Klaxon horn. And there was the distant growl and whine of speeding motors. The echo of distant explosions increased.

High overhead, planes whose cargo had been dropped, droned away toward England. And everywhere antiaircraft fire was spitting even more frantically.

Who were these men dangling from parachutes? If they had started the Invasion, all Maquis ought to help them. "Then that means me, too," André thought.

He braced his foot in the crotch of the tree, lowered the other to feel his way down.

He dropped to another branch—and it snapped!

Just then the moon sailed from under a cloud and touched him as brightly as a searchlight.

A hoarse cry came from a few feet away. "Look out! Sniper in that tree!"

André saw the glint of the gun barrel swinging up toward him.

But a louder voice from the man dangling in the tree shouted, *"Hold it.* Hold it, Slim. It's just a kid. I can see him. Don't shoot. Say, somebody come over here and cut me down."

André's stiffened body relaxed, and he began to feel his way among the dim branches. Several men had gathered at the foot of the tree, whispering, and one of them lifted his voice angrily. "What's a kid doin' in a tree this time of night? Something funny here."

"Okay. *Okay.* We'll find out. But get me down before this harness cuts me in two."

André called, "Don't shoot me. I'm coming down. I want to help."

He slithered more quickly now from limb to limb, and jumped. Instantly a flashlight blinded him, and a drawling voice said, "Well, what d'ya know! A little shrimp!"

The flashlight had been turned to the ground. As soon as his eyes had grown accustomed to it, André gaped at the men. Never had he seen such frightening figures: torn uniforms, faces blackened with soot, each one bristling with every kind of small arm and grenade, topped off by helmets festooned with leafy twigs.

He gasped in amazement. "Are you Americans?"

The most tattered of the men grinned. "Sure. Who you expecting? Say, how come you're talking English?"

"My sister and I learned a lot of English from Father Duprey," André replied, "just in case."

"Case of what?" demanded the suspicious one.

[*44*]

"To help you when you came," said André. "But sir, shouldn't we get that man up there out of the tree?"

"It's about time!" came from the branches near by.

André shinnied quickly up above the dangling trooper and disentangled the chute. A moment later the chutist was on the ground, unstrapping his Tommy gun.

A stocky, bristling soldier had been looking out over the highway uneasily. Now he said, "Say, Slim, we gotta get movin'. We're supposed to get to the causeways across the flooded part. Give 'em the signal, Risso."

Softly then, André heard a little rasping cricket-sound that was repeated almost at once from the meadow.

More helmeted men crept up to the group. They said, "Hi, Sarge, what now?"

The stocky sergeant had been studying the darkened scene around him. Now he said, "We're too far inland." He looked down at André. "Listen, kid. You really mean you want to help us Americans—you aren't up to no tricks?"

André frowned. "I've been waiting to help for a long time. It is my country here."

The sergeant's face softened a little. "Okay, I believe you. But listen. Where's your folks?"

"My family has gone away," André explained.

[45]

"But they'll be home soon. What do you want me to do?"

"You just tell us how far it is to the nearest road across that lagoon—"

Andre interrupted excitedly, "First, I must tell you, there are at least six Nazis in our barn. They have machine guns trained on the road. I'll show you the way around the back wall. You could catch them from behind."

The sergeant stiffened. "You, Slim, stay here with the kid, out of range—and both of you *keep down*," he ordered.

Several shapes moved quietly off into the black field.

André looked up at the gray shape of the lean, rangy fellow slouched against a tree. The soldier held his Tommy gun easily. A thumb was hooked in the belt festooned with grenades, and a wicked-looking sheath knife was strapped to his leg.

André cleared his throat and asked, "Slim—is this the—Invasion?"

The paratrooper smiled. "Well, son," he drawled, "it's a start, anyhow. Quite a parcel of us has been dropped from Heaven, and I reckon there'll be an awful lot more tomorrow when the gliders get in. All I know is, son, I'm a long, long way from Pecos, Texas."

After that, for a moment, André thought the man was going to sleep. Presently he noticed that the trooper's face was half turned away and that he was listening intently.

A dog barked, and André cried softly, "That's my Patchou. The men must be coming into our farmyard."

Suddenly, an explosion of shots, grenades, and hoarse shouts came from the direction of the house.

"Got 'em," sighed Slim. "They're good, our boys are. Especially at that sneaky stuff. Better keep down there. Might be bullets flyin' 'round. I *do not* like flyin' bullets."

As the racket continued, the two stretched out among the ferns. "May's well rest," Slim murmured drowsily. "Doubt if there's gonna be much time from now on."

A few moments later there was a crackling in the hedge, from a direction away from the farm.

Slim shot into action like a snake, Tommy gun aimed, body tense. The faint sounds continued. After a moment Slim called, "Halt! You out there. Stay where you are."

A gusty sigh came through the undergrowth, and then a voice. "You from the 505th?"

Slim kept his gun steady and answered, "Check. Who're you?"

There was a soft groan. "Captain Dobie."

Slim stared at the man pushing toward them, then sprang forward.

"You hurt, sir?" He helped the officer to get to his feet and took his arm. With André on the other side, they helped him stagger into the shadow of a tree.

"We thought we'd lost you sure, Cap'n," Slim said sympathetically.

"Broke my leg when I landed on a stone wall, I guess," the officer said fretfully. He stared around him and asked, "What's happening? We should start toward the coast—we're much too far in."

Slim nodded. "I know. But Sergeant Weller's cleanin' out a machine gun nest in the barn yonder. He'll be back with six or seven men shortly. They must have finished over there by now. Some Nazis was in this kid's barn." Slim directed a long thumb at André, and added, "He's puny, but he's real sharp."

In spite of the fact that he was evidently in great pain, the captain managed to smile at the boy.

Slim had helped him to sit down, braced against the tree. André saw that he was watching—Slim, André himself, the road, the meadow. And he was listening to the distant noises—for the return of his men.

"Should be nearly a hundred men in these meadows right here," the captain said. "We've got to get our parachuted equipment together. As soon as you can, send someone for gear I saw drop near where I came down. One lot's caught in a tree—right across that open space. We need those bazookas quick. German tanks are likely to be coming along any minute."

"This kid might be able to tell us somethin' about the Nazis around these parts," Slim said.

"There's a Nazi camp half a mile down the road," André replied eagerly. "And another big one near Ste. Mère Église, if you know where that is."

Captain Dobie nodded and turned his head to catch the sound of a motor. "That car's coming this way fast!"

André was startled by the smooth swiftness with which Slim and his captain acted then. Thrusting his Tommy gun into the captain's outstretched hand without a word, Slim detached a grenade from the cluster at his belt. He slipped into a tense, waiting position closer to the road.

The captain ordered, "Down flat!" and André obeyed.

The roar of the approaching car grew loud. Slim called softly, over his shoulder, "Nazi staff car," and raised his arm.

The explosion and the repeated crack of the Tommy gun beside him shook the ground under André. As another grenade followed the first and took effect, Captain Dobie said, "That's one car won't stop the freeing of France."

Slim crossed the road and returned to report solemnly, "Okay, sir."

The captain nodded, then glanced quickly to one side as a voice said, "Good work, Slim."

"Oh, it's you, Sergeant!" the captain exclaimed in relief.

"Captain," Weller said. "We were worried about you. What you got there?"

"A broken leg, I think, worse luck," Captain Dobie explained angrily. "If you see a medic, send him back here. But you men get going now. If we don't pick up that dropped ammunition and equipment soon, we may be in for trouble. Meanwhile, have you seen any place I can use for a command post around here?"

"You can use my father's house," André offered eagerly. "My father, he's a part of the Resistance, so it's all right."

The captain turned to Weller.

"Yes, sir. Solid stone, handy to the road, plenty of room, barns. No bomb damage," the sergeant reported, and added, "Nobody but this kid home, since we cleaned out the loft."

"Yes?" The captain looked sharply around at the boy. "How's that?"

André explained quickly. "And my father and Marie should have come back by now," he finished.

The captain shook his head. "Not from St. Sauveur, they won't. Not tonight. Our men must have all the roads beyond Ste. Mère blocked off."

While a couple of men watched the road, others were sent to retrieve the dropped weapons. Sergeant Weller examined the captain's injury. He found that a bone was cracked above the ankle. A shot of morphine from a first-aid kit was given Captain Dobie to ease the pain. Then splints were found, and the leg bound with strips of torn parachute silk.

Halfway through this, Weller paused suddenly and said to André, "By the way, son, you better tie up that hound of yours. He doesn't seem to know Americans are his friends, by the way he lit into my only pair of britches."

The little party moved slowly toward the Gagnon house, helping the half-crippled captain.

Pale moonlight glowed on the windows and against dark walls. When André saw the front door ajar, he cried happily, "They must have come home while I was asleep."

" 'Fraid not." the sergeant corrected. "We went through the whole house—André. Want to know how I got your name?" Weller grinned. "Read Marie's note about your supper on the kitchen table."

Immediately inside the house, the sergeant said crisply, "This room okay, Captain? I guess it's a sort of store during peacetime. I'll get you a table and somethin' to sit on, pronto."

André had run to light candles and draw the blackout curtains. Then he dragged his mother's best velvet chair from the parlor for Captain Dobie, and brought cushions to prop up his leg.

Captain Dobie spread maps on the table before him, but paused to study the boy.

André looked into his kind, thoughtful face and asked, "Do you think my father and sister will be all right, sir? It would be awful. . . ."

The captain nodded. "Nobody'd let them start out from St. Sauveur tonight, son. They'll be all right."

But André's worry was not so easily talked away. The thud of bombs and firing inland was too continuous.

He heard a whine and rushed into the kitchen to a wet, pawing welcome from Patchou. He tugged at the familiar warm fur and when Patchou had calmed down, brought him a bowl of milk. Then, with a warning to be quiet, he chained the dog to the fireplace grate.

At the front of the house he found that a strange, businesslike disorder was mounting.

Just inside the door, bazookas, mortars, and ammunition of all sorts were being pulled from "drop" bundles. Bulky, helmeted soldiers were coming in from everywhere, receiving quick orders from the captain, and clanking off in groups. Captain Dobie sent out a messenger for a walkie-talkie, to make contact with his commanding colonel.

At one moment, everyone around the captain paused warily as the roar of a low-flying plane shook the walls. Sergeant Weller and André darted out to the doorway and stared up at the U. S. markings. As the plane sped by, a shower of paper cascaded over the town.

"That's one of our Flying Fortresses dropping leaflets, telling the Frenchies to scatter 'n stay off the roads." Weller shrugged. "That means you, too, boy, y'know."

For the next thirty minutes André sat and watched while dirty, hot men clumped in and out on errands that made no sense to him. Some had been wounded. Many, hurt in the jump, were being treated both by medics and some of the village people. Slim pushed his way into the room, looking leaner and sootier than ever—all his drowsiness gone.

André listened to his report. More troops were needed at once toward the causeways. Glider troops had landed, but the Germans were putting up a fierce fight. The Americans wanted all the reinforcements they could get rushed up fast.

Captain Dobie turned to Weller. "Okay, Sergeant, take *all* these men. It's our job to wipe out those bridgeheads!" When Weller hesitated, he snapped, "What're you waiting for?"

The sergeant blinked. "And leave you here alone, sir?"

"We've *got* to get those bridgeheads. Move!" Captain Dobie pounded the table. "Orders!"

Sergeant Weller turned on his heel, shouted commands to round up all the men, and left.

But just outside the door he jerked Slim aside. "You stay," he ordered. "I'm not gonna leave the cap'n here alone with a broken leg. What would he do if some Nazis came along?"

"You'll get me courtmartialed yet, Sarge," Slim objected.

"If you don't beat me to it. Stay out of sight."

The sergeant barked a command, and guns and men moved away through the mud.

It was nearly full daylight now. When André turned back into the house he saw by the clock that it was quarter to six.

What would his family say if they knew he had not been to bed at all? He wondered sleepily whether to lie down quietly in a corner.

The captain was looking at his watch.

André had taken a step toward him when the house was shaken under a dreadful blast of sound.

The sound rose, and he realized it came from the sea. Under the thud of heavy shelling and bombing, objects on the walls and tables danced.

The captain looked up from his watch and smiled.

"They're right on time," he said.

Puzzled, André asked, "Who is, monsieur?"

"This is the *real* Invasion, son, coming in now. This is what General Eisenhower has been planning for two years. Hundreds of thousands of men, tens of thousands of tanks, bulldozers, and trucks are moving in—*now,* in over four thousand ships. The Navy's shelling the coast. We just came in ahead by parachute to get ready for them."

André found himself too excited to say anything.

The captain spoke again, above the din.

"You see why we have to clear the enemy out of those bridgeheads? To let the men landing on the beaches come through. As soon as the Navy finishes this shelling, British, Canadian, and American troops will be landing on sixty miles of beach from here to the River Orne!"

CHAPTER SIX

Victor's Mission

REMEMBERING the rolling crashes of the worst thunderstorm he had ever heard, André thought it had been nothing compared to this noise.

He braced himself by the door frame and looked toward the sea. A pall of dense, black smoke was drifting inland, blotting out the newly risen sun. Fires flared over the tree tops.

He saw Slim grinning back at him from behind a thick lilac bush.

On the other side of the road, the Lescots' front door opened. Victor, in nightcap and corduroy pants drawn over a blue nightshirt, darted out, picked up one of the dropped leaflets, and shot back into the house.

From other houses people ran out and raced away into the fields.

Bombers darted in and out of the curtain of

smoke. A barn less than a mile away broke into flames.

Through a lull in the battle sounds André heard the outraged moo of a cow.

"Poor old beasts," André thought, "they must be scared to death. I'll go talk to them, and milk."

He looked again for Slim and saw that he had turned his back to the fury of the coast and was staring toward Ste. Mère. As André stepped out Slim whirled and shouted, "Tell the cap'n—two Nazi tanks comin' this way!"

But André had already heard the ominous clank of the tanks. Even through the battle sounds their threat rang out—a new danger.

As Slim raced toward him, André broke into a run for the house, shouting, "TANKS, mon Capitaine. Nazi tanks coming!"

Captain Dobie had risen and stumbled a step toward the window.

"Blast it!" he shouted. "Help me, Cimino."

André then saw a new man in the room—a soldier with a walkie-talkie, who must have arrived by way of the farmyard.

Slim plunged through the door and snatched up a bazooka from the pile of arms in the hall. Cimino, the walkie-talkie operator, slipped out of the straps holding the instrument. He flung himself toward Slim to serve as second man on the bazooka.

"Help me to the window, André," Captain Dobie ordered, picking up a Tommy gun. "Then stay out of range.

"Slim," he barked, "fire at the front drive sprocket and the gas tanks, center, low. You can't penetrate that forward armor, remember."

The bazooka muzzle thrust out the window, Slim knelt in tense firing position. Cimino stood ready to reload.

The captain braced himself at the second window, Tommy gun leveled. André heard the rumble of the tanks draw nearer.

The explosion of fire from the windows and the fierce back-flash of the bazooka joined with the grinding screech of shattered metal, outside.

Then came the hollow scraping of steel on steel.

Over Slim's head André had seen the first tank's turret. Then the second tank tottered over the first. And like a huge apple peel, a tremendous snakelike steel tread whipped through the air.

"Good," snapped Captain Dobie. "Second one's piled up on the first. Shoot overhead, once."

When the firing from the house stopped, there came a shout of *"Kamerad!"*

The captain poked his weapon farther out the window and shouted, "Get out and put your hands up fast. You're all covered. Okay, Slim, get your prisoners."

Cimino stacked the bazooka against the sill, and whipped out his .45 automatic. Slim swept up a carbine and strode outside.

The crews were already out of the tanks.

"All right. Hands on your heads!" Slim shouted.

As his captives moved toward him, Cimino lifted their side arms from holsters, pushing the prisoners swiftly toward the house.

"Get in there, quick," Slim commanded.

He had only just herded them into the hall when his voice was drowned out by the explosion of the gas tanks in one of the wrecked vehicles.

The captain and André ducked as ammunition, set off by the flames, sprayed the outside of the house.

When it was over, the captain leaned out the window, and André asked, "Did it wreck my father's pump?"

"Just knocked down the sign that said 'Chocolate,'" the captain said.

"That's all right," André laughed shakily. "We did not have any left to sell, anyway."

Captain Dobie wiped the sweat from his face, and with André's help, hobbled back to his easy chair and cushions.

The Germans, lined up against the wall, stared at him silently, open-mouthed.

"Are there any more tanks coming this way?" demanded the captain.

One of the Nazis, with sergeant's stripes, said, "*Nein*—no more," with surly shortness.

"Be respectful," snapped the captain coldly. He turned to Slim. "Take them out to the yard and stand guard, Slim," he said. "Cimino, try to raise someone on the talkie. If you can't, get a runner to locate the colonel and tell him where *we* are."

After several minutes, Cimino reported, "Some sergeant thinks our colonel's over near the first bridgehead. He'll pass the word along."

André, at the captain's suggestion, went out to survey the road and report any sight of the enemy. "Here, take my helmet," offered the captain. "There's too much stuff falling out of the sky."

The thud of heavy explosions beyond the village continued to rock the earth.

André had been on watch but a few minutes when he sighted a car. He called back through the window, "Jeep coming, sir—from the coast."

Slim, who had been relieved of his guard duty by Cimino, rushed out to join André.

The little car swung in toward the two, and braked with a screech. Slim shouted, "Weller! Where'ja get that!"

Sergeant Weller was eyeing the wrecked German tanks.

"Well, Texas," he smiled approvingly, "good thing I left you here."

He slid out of the seat. "Lucky those two tanks

didn't get through to hit us from behind," he said. "We've sure had our hands full down there. The Heinies came at us from all sides. But, for some reason, one of the causeways across the swamps was unguarded."

"We got some prisoners for you, out back," Slim announced. "And you better report to the cap'n," he added. "He's restless as a hungry puppy. Ain't had a word from anybody higher up. Didn't come across our colonel, did you?"

"That's what I came back for," said Weller. "Saw him and told him about this command post. He's feelin' good. We've taken two bridgeheads."

"But *where* did you get the jeep?" André asked.

Weller patted the mud-splattered windshield. "I 'liberated' her from a smashed glider, son." He turned a thumb to the heaps of K-rations packed in the rear of the jeep. "Near time we ate," he said. "But, right now, I'm in need of gas, kid. I bet you got some in that pump."

"A little," André said.

Slim and Weller clanked off to the house while André connected the hose to the jeep tank and began to pump. His eyelids were drooping.

It takes a long time for this Invasion to get going, he thought. He had already grown used to the *thrump* of big artillery, the bark of machine and rifle fire scattered across all of Normandy. He had heard Cimino say that the 82nd Airborne were getting on well around Ste. Mère, though the Germans were fighting bitterly. The Liberation was too big. André could think of it no more.

And through his weariness he heard the cows again. Milking time was long past. In the barn the cows turned their sad eyes on him accusingly. He rested his forehead on their soft, warm bodies while he milked, and both he and the frightened beasts were soothed. He saw to it that they had fresh hay and water. The open pasture was no place for them today.

Finally the job was done; the last of his strength was gone. He put the pails of milk to one side and sank into a pile of fresh straw.

"I'll take them to the springhouse in a minute," he promised himself. And he wriggled flat in the fragrant hay and spread out his arms peacefully.

All battle sounds were muffled by the thick old stone walls. The familiar rustle and stamping of cattle were like a familiar song. . . .

He woke with a hand shaking his shoulder.

Someone was saying, in French, "Wake up, André. Wake up! The *Invasion* has started."

André opened his eyes and saw Victor Lescot bent over him.

"Shame on you, André," he scolded. "Milk getting sour. War going on all around, and you sleeping."

André sat up. "You're supposed to be shut up in your house, Victor. What are you doing here?" he said crossly.

"I can't stay home now," Victor bristled. "I've got to go get my new cart—before it is destroyed."

Now wide awake, André said with disgust, "You can't go out into the fighting."

"But I *must*," Victor interrupted shrilly. "My new cart will be blown to bits if I leave it at Jacquard's. Then what?"

André could not believe his ears. "Would you rather be blown to bits yourself?" he demanded.

"But we do not need to thrust ourselves into danger," Victor protested. "We'll make our way to Jacquard's village by the cowpaths, you and I. We know them well, eh?"

"*WE?*" André echoed. "*Who's* going with you?"

"But you, naturally, my little friend, I may need you to speak English."

"Where is the cart?" André asked.

"At Jacquard's workshop, on his farm. I have told you about it on numerous occasions."

André smiled. "Victor Lescot, Jacquard's shop is right near the coast, where the fighting is. Who knows, there may be a battle going on in Jacquard's own courtyard right now."

Victor's eyes flickered. "Ah, but I have a plan."

"There is no sense to it." André shrugged and got to his feet.

"No sense!" Victor cried, as though he were about to hurl a bolt of lightning. "You forget. The cart is *mine. I paid for it* yesterday."

Again André could only shake his head.

"I'll put this milk where it is cool," he said, and started off with a pail in each hand.

Victor dived for the other pail and followed. "La Fumée, my mare that you have always been so fond of, you know," he chattered, "she's all harnessed and impatient to start off. You know how she loves adventure."

Just then there was a definite lull in the shelling. André set the pails into the cool, stone-lined spring, taking Victor's from him.

Victor caught his eye. "The noise is not so loud," he said. "There is a trifling din, true, but it is less."

"Perhaps the worst is over," André said. "We could just start out, and if they tell us we can't proceed, we can turn back . . ."

Victor's pink face crinkled brightly. "But of course. Anything else would be gross stupidity."

André fretted: Now he thinks I've promised to get his cart no matter what happens.

But the Americans would turn them back at once—so no harm would be done.

"Okay, Victor. I will start out," he said.

CHAPTER SEVEN

Tricolor over Ste. Mère

Andŕé hesitated. "You wait for me at your house," he said. "First, I have one thing to do."

Victor stole a searching glance at the boy, then, almost reassured, he nodded and left the springhouse at once.

André filled a pitcher with milk and started for the kitchen door.

Ranged along the barnyard wall lounged half a hundred German prisoners surrounded by a semi-circle of muddy guards bristling with carbines and Tommy guns.

André found a mug in the kitchen, and carried the milk in to Captain Dobie.

He noticed that the officer's leg was badly swollen, but the captain seemed unaware of it.

The room was crammed with soldiers. Several neighbors, men and women, pressed through the crowd, begging to give help. Many wounded villagers lay sheltered under the trees, they said. But they and the small neighborhood children were being cared for and fed. The captain welcomed them and advised the elders to get deep cellars ready. They must keep the children close to them in case the fighting broke out in the village.

"The Germans are fighting hard everywhere, and we must silence each Nazi gun no matter where we find it," he explained. "Until we get a solid foothold here, we cannot help liberate your country."

André listened, and when he caught the captain's eye, offered his jug of milk. With a grateful smile, Dobie drained the jug thirstily.

"Are things going all right, sir?" André asked.

The captain seemed reluctant to reply. But after a moment he said, "The landings are the hardest, son. The Nazis made the coast tough with their underwater obstructions, and the sea has been a lot rougher than we'd planned on. But it's going along well. You ought to be seeing heavy equipment coming along the roads soon."

Sergeant Weller clumped in with two soldiers and a battle-weary young Frenchman. "Look, kid," Weller shouted to André. "D'you know who this character is? I can't make head or tail what he's sayin'. *He* says he's speakin' English, but, boy, it's nothin' I ever heard in Brooklyn."

[67]

The young Frenchman called to André in French, "You are Pierre's son, no? Tell them quickly who I am. Make them see my urgency, I beg you."

André looked at the man's flashing eyes, the beaked nose, the shock of dark hair.

"Yes, I know him," he said quickly. "This is François, the famous Maquis leader. You can trust him."

"You sure?" Weller demanded.

"I'm sure," André said. "I have seen him and heard my father describe him often. One moment—"

In French, François told André his story: "I was coming to your father to get more Resistance help. My band is too small. We discovered Nazis coming up behind your father's orchard with a mobile gun. They are going to blow up this house because it is an American headquarters."

"Translate so far," Weller said, and André obeyed.

Weller scowled. "Yeh? Well, in that case . . ."

He made his way to the captain, and a moment later André heard him shouting orders.

When Weller returned he put out both hands and the Frenchman shook them warmly.

The squad Weller was forming was hastily gathering up grenades, bazookas, and other equipment.

André asked the Maquis anxiously, "Can you tell me anything about St. Sauveur? How is the battle going beyond Ste. Mère?"

François looked solemn, but answered quickly. "St. Sauveur, we think, is still mostly outside the fighting. Not all of Ste. Mère has been cleared of Germans yet. But the center of the town is under control. At least, the Americans have the French flag flying from Ste. Mère Église's town hall. None of the Allied tanks have come through yet and they are badly needed. Also, in some places the Americans are running short of ammunition. And the Nazis are building up their forces near the bridges over the Merderet River, west of Ste. Mère."

He broke off at Weller's signal, and with the sergeant's squad slipped out through the barnyard.

"The French flag flying from Ste. Mère Église's town hall!" André repeated it aloud. And a familiar voice at the doorway echoed the great words.

Raoul Cotein stood just outside the door. His arm and forehead were bandaged, and in his hand was a package wrapped in a napkin.

He took a step forward. "My wife—well, she is troubled because your mother and sister are not here. If you will just accept these few sandwiches?"

André took the packet with a puzzled "Thank

The squad gathered up grenades, bazookas, and other equipment

you," and stared at his suddenly subdued neighbor.

"W-what happened to you?" he asked.

Raoul looked down at his arm bandage. "You mean this?" he replied. *"Tiens,* André. Do you know, I found I was almost the only man in this village who was not of the Resistance? I have merely been remedying the situation."

"Do you know now my father is a Maquis and not a collaborationist?" André demanded, and Raoul nodded. "I have discovered so. I—"

If he had meant to apologize further for his past bad behavior, his words were lost. A shell overshot the house and everyone ran for cover.

When André slid out from his hiding place, Raoul was gone.

For a moment the boy stood alone. "Well, now, what is my duty?" he considered. "Victor? No. . . . Patchou."

He went to the kitchen, gave the dog food and water, and hastily ate Raoul's sandwiches. Meanwhile Patchou gamboled for a few minutes around the room.

André thought that he had better go to Lescots' and tell the old man, once and for all, how foolish his plan was. Even Victor would see that now.

Victor stood near his barnyard gates crossly watching the distant scene.

A broad, fawn-colored Percheron stood harnessed beside Victor. A shotgun was strapped to the horse's back-pad alongside the looped-up traces.

André slipped over the wall and whistled.

At the sound, Victor jumped, steadied his glasses, and chattered, "Oh, it's you at last. La Fumée is beside herself with impatience."

André interrupted firmly. "I came only to tell you the thought of going toward the coast is an insanity. The fighting has grown intense."

Victor fanned out his hands. "Then my cart . . . you think it is a trifle to be ignored. . . ." His eyes snapped. "Which *I have paid for,* please recall!"

"But Victor—" André sighed.

"From infancy I have indulged you, because of my love . . ." Victor chided gently.

He patted the mare's smooth flank and climbed up on her back. "There will be many Americans down there, I presume. No doubt they will help an old man."

"Victor, you know I can't let you go alone," André exploded. "Pull me up behind you."

A few moments later, André, clinging to Victor's ribs, was mounted and jogging around a corner of the farm wall.

CHAPTER EIGHT

Prisoners

As a very small boy, riding on the broad platform of La Fumée's back had been André's delight. But La Fumée had not then quivered at the whine and roar of shells, or the nerve-shaking rattle of machine guns. And the fields had not been spiked with wicked barbed-wire glider traps.

"Now, we zigzag," explained Victor as he turned the mare into a hedge-lined path at the next field. It was necessary to round barns and ponds and areas marked in German: *"Achtung— Minen!"* "Beware—Mines!" to avoid even the smaller country roads.

They covered nearly a mile at the Percheron's steady plod. Then a shell crashed a hundred yards away, and the horse cowered under a shower of falling debris. Victor and André had flattened themselves on the Percheron's vast back. With his head still buried in Victor's rough coat, André begged, "Surely it is wiser to turn back, Victor."

The old man sighed. "But it is now such a little way. It is a pity."

Both sat up cautiously.

The marshes glowed beyond a broken orchard, just across the Paris-Cherbourg road. Far to the northeast, from a German pillbox sunk beside the flooded land, swiveled guns thumped, and were immediately answered by other, unseen guns.

Before they could move again, André cried, "Listen!"

A tremendous explosion, close to the sea, was followed by a shattering series of rolling reverberations. And immediately, from almost on the horizon, a fleet of planes swept upward sharply over their heads.

"Dive bombers," André cried. "They must be finishing off those big German guns on the sea bluff."

Then, added to the shock and noise of the bombing, rose all around them a fury of gobbling protest. Turkeys which had been roosting in the trees screamed and fluttered insanely. In the grass, a family of small white pigs ran helter-skelter toward the hedges.

La Fumée stood stiff, with rolling eyes.

At length the last wave of bombers passed. The air over the orchard reeked, and smoke seeped inland from the marshes.

The turkeys continued to scold, their voices dropping to an angry gurgle.

"There, that is over," Victor said firmly. "Jacquard's is so close, we may as well go on."

La Fumée moved woodenly, and André smoothed her thick, firm flank with a gentle hand.

If they were to go on, they must cross the wide, pitted Paris-Cherbourg road. And into this angled a smaller one. This led to Jacquard's, and continued seaward to the hamlet of l'Audouville.

The road stretching north and south was completely deserted just then except for a litter of wrecked Nazi trucks pushed to the sides.

La Fumée put on a jiggling burst of speed to cross the main road. The smaller road also seemed empty.

"You see," Victor said. "Here we are. Jacquard's place is just ahead."

André's sharper eyes studied the high stone walls and the slate roofs above. "It has been bombed or shelled already," he said.

Victor hunched forward, shocked into silence.

The farm's roadside gates sagged open on broken hinges, and fowl wandered in and out.

The sound of a car racing up the main road to Cherbourg caught André's ear. As he turned, he saw the car hesitate at the fork of their road, and then swing into it at gathering speed.

He thrust his hand under Victor's arm, grabbed the reins, and yanked the Percheron into the shallow ditch at the side.

The car swept past so fast, André caught only a glimpse of the Nazi Swastika on the side.

Nearing the broken gate, the Nazi driver slowed uncertainly. But instantly he swung into a teetering turn, and shot into the barnyard in the midst of an uproar of cackling hens and geese.

There was a muffled crash.

André and Victor slid quickly from La Fumée's back with thumping hearts.

"They are trapped," André whispered, "and do not know how to get out. We must bring some soldiers before they come out."

Victor was loosening his shotgun with trembling hands. But his experience with farmyards now served him well.

"Without a doubt, those Nazi officers have run spank into the manure pile," he stated with satisfaction. "They will find some troublesomeness getting loose." He took a step forward. "You must run quickly for help."

André thought, "The first of the soldiers from the landing barges must surely be coming across the causeways by now. Captain Dobie said they would."

Skittering along past the gate into the grassy edge of the road, he began to run toward l'Audouville as fast as his legs would carry him.

Racing against time, André could not look back. Before he reached the turn his heart leaped.

A soldier, bulky with equipment, was coming toward him. He was moving cautiously along the roadside, rifle poised. And fanning out behind him was a spaced line of Americans.

André dashed toward them.

Unsmiling and with leveled gun, the first soldier yelled, "Halt!" He then said rapidly in French, "Who are you? And *where're* you going?"

André pointed back to the Jacquard farm. "Nazi officers back there. Come get them quick— please."

Beckoning, he turned to run.

[77]

"Just a minute there," the soldier shouted. "Come back here, *petit garçon*. What's this you're talking about?"

André was terrified by the wasted minutes.

He shouted, *"Come!* A car full of Nazi officers just drove into a farmyard back there. *Hurry!* You can take them, but *hurry."*

The scattered scouting party began to move ahead warily.

"It's a chance the kid is okay," the sergeant called back. "We'll have to take a look. Keep your eyes open—and keep separated."

The sergeant quickened his pace, but cautioned, "Take it easy, kid. Let us get 'em."

Before they reached the Jacquard gate, sheltered by bushes, André fell to his knees and crept toward it.

He had not quite reached it when two quick shotgun blasts rang out.

"That's Victor's gun," he said. "The Nazis must have started to leave."

Shot rattled on metal, and the tail of the Nazi car smashed through the gates. But, halfway through, the car teetered sharply into the stone post. Rocking, it toppled over and skidded to a stop.

A voice shouted toward the car, "Hold it. Get out and keep your hands up!" A Tommy gun chattered across the car's spinning wheels.

Scrambling boots pounded into action. The German officers were jerked up and out through the door. André was startled to see a colonel's insignia on one officer's shoulders.

When the Nazis were all on their feet, the sergeant's men surrounded them. Two soldiers relieved the officers of their side arms.

As the shock of their capture wore off, the Nazis began to protest curtly, and the sergeant retorted in their own language.

"Okay. You're staff officers! We'll get you to the proper authorities just as soon as we can."

André had seen plenty of Germans, but few of such high rank.

Suddenly it dawned on him that it was Victor's shots which had made the capture possible by wrecking the car. But where was Victor?

André ran around the farm buildings, but neither Victor nor La Fumée was in sight—anywhere.

Shells had blasted the carpentry shop, and rubbish lay over the scattered, twisted, and blackened tools.

After a thorough search, André stumbled sadly out to the courtyard and around the scattered manure pile, toward the group at the gate.

He was greeted by a shout from a jeep which had driven up. "Hi, there. You—boy!"

An American lieutenant sat at the wheel, with

the two Nazi officers crammed rigidly in the rear seat. An American with a Tommy gun perched backward on each of the front mudguards, and the German driver, his arm in a sling, shared the front seat with the lieutenant.

Impatiently, the lieutenant asked André whether he knew where the nearest U. S. headquarters had been set up.

André pointed up the road and replied, with some pride, that there was an 82nd Command Post in his own house. "It's a little more than a mile up that way," he said.

The lieutenant grinned. "Well, hop in and show us the way."

André stood stubbornly firm. "But Lieutenant," he protested, "I came with Victor. He's an old man. I can't leave him here."

"*Get in,*" snapped the lieutenant. "You can find him later. There's a war on."

"As if I didn't know," André thought crossly.

But he climbed over the great booted legs of the guard, and hunched in under the elbow of the German prisoner.

The jeep lurched into gear and roared down the road.

CHAPTER NINE

Victor Disappears

As THE jeep bumped rapidly along, André explained to the lieutenant, "I didn't want to leave there, sir, till I found my friend Victor. He was the one who really stopped that Nazi car, shooting at the tires, I think."

"He did?" the lieutenant exclaimed. "Well, why did he disappear after we got there?"

One of the guards interrupted. "Old Frenchman? Walrus mustache? With a shotgun?"

André nodded excitedly. "Did you see him?"

"Saw a man like that run back into the orchard of that farm just as we came up."

André said no more; at least Victor could run.

The jeep had been proceeding cautiously around road blocks and paratroopers. Now it speeded up.

A little while later, André saw the roofs of his

own village, and he cried, "Oh! it's been hit!"

It was a different village than the one André had left. Many shells must have struck it. Trees were shattered and old walls tumbled. Two houses, not far from the Gagnons', were badly damaged—one lay in smoking ruins.

People of the neighborhood shuffled to and fro with arms filled with possessions.

André called to one of them, "The Cotys and Mme. Lescot—are they all right?"

"Yes. Everyone did what your captain told us to. We ran into the fields and hid in ditches when those German shells started coming. It was not for long. We are told the Maquis found the Nazi gun and blew it up."

At a sign from André, the jeep slowed and, a moment later, he saw that his father's house still stood.

In the doorway, Sergeant Weller shouted at sight of the jeep.

"Kid, you had us scared. Where the—where you been?" he demanded tartly of André. But he did not wait for an answer.

He gave the jeep and its load a hasty glance, and cried, "*You* bringin' in prisoners, too!" Then, noticing their rank, he added to the lieutenant, in his sharp, official bark, "Bring that German 'brass' right in here, sir. Our company colonel's inside. He'll sure want to question 'em."

Inside the house André found a new, older American officer busy with maps beside Captain Dobie.

They received the prisoners coolly.

After questioning the Nazi officers a few moments, Captain Dobie hobbled out to the hallway and closed the door after him. His broken leg wore fresh splints and a new dressing.

The captain looked at André with displeasure. "I should keep a closer eye on you, boy," he said sharply. "What do you mean by running loose around the country with a war going on?"

Before the captain could continue, Slim sidled through the doorway.

"Excuse me, sir," he said, "but that lieutenant an' the guards are sittin' out there in the jeep.

D'ya want 'em to wait, or can they go, the lieutenant says?"

A call from the colonel in the other room, summoning Captain Dobie, interrupted him.

When Dobie returned with the colonel, the Nazis, well covered by guns, were ceremoniously marched back to the jeep.

The American officer's orders were curt. "Lieutenant, I want these men delivered to the general, by you, personally. He's somewhere on Utah Beach by now."

The jeep, loaded like a school bus, turned and disappeared in the direction from which it had just come.

CHAPTER TEN

"Here Come the Tanks!"

LONG before dark, André, too tired to care any more what happened, had stumbled into his old bed in the kitchen. During the night he roused at times to hear the hum of trucks and clumping feet. He did not hear the squadrons of planes coming in to drop relief troops and much-needed ammunition to the hard-pressed 'chutists.

At dawn he awoke completely fresh, and went to look at his now unfamiliar Normandy landscape.

Women tramped to damaged houses, distributing hot food and blankets. Two small boys were investigating a badly smashed glider which had settled on a hedge.

André had just decided to run to the Lescot farm, to inquire whether Victor had come home, when Weller called to him to come to breakfast.

[86]

Afterwards, he went about his usual farm chores.

Troops from the beach landings filtered through the village that day. Their officers paused briefly at the Gagnon house to exchange reports with Captain Dobie.

"Well, at any rate, our tanks are beginning to come across the causeways now," a newly arrived major told the captain. "That'll help the airborne boys."

"It will be a great relief," Captain Dobie said. "Our parachute fellows have been fighting hard without any rest."

The major nodded. "The only trouble is," he said, "somebody overlooked the way these thick French hedgerows stop our tanks cold. We've got to find a way to cut through them."

André listened with amazement. He had never thought of those ancient borders to the tiny Normandy meadows as tank traps. He knew, of course, that cattle turned out to pasture seldom broke through the high, earth banks topped by the century-old tangles. It did seem disappointing to think that those great, wonderful American war machines could be stopped by shrubbery.

"But why don't the tanks keep to the roads, sir?" he asked.

The major grinned. "If Normandy had ten times as many roads, son," he replied, "we wouldn't have enough for all the stuff the Allies have to move into France. Besides, our tanks have to go where we know the Germans are massing."

The major was right about over-busy highways.

Trucks, loaded with armed men and supplies, had begun to grind by in a long, noisy procession. Some village people had come back from hiding. Children big and little ran along the roadside, catching windfalls of candy, gum, and cellophane-wrapped cookies tossed out by the soldiers.

To André this was a very, very strange war—he could remember nothing like it in any history book.

But when he went into the kitchen, he no longer felt that his father's house was threatened from all sides.

The crowd of German prisoners had been moved to a new compound, and the geese had once more taken possession of the pond. André counted the chickens. The flock looked a little sparse.

A shout from Sergeant Weller sent André back to the road.

Inside the front window Captain Dobie and Slim stood, waving cheerily. Weller, both arms upraised, was saluting the approach of a great elephant of a machine. It came lumbering up the sea road, its wide, corrugated treads clanking on the gravel. After the first, in stately dignity, thundered more of the metallic herd.

"The TANKS! The tanks!"

André's heart thumped with excitement.

"Some sight, eh, boy?" Weller shouted.

With Weller, André ran out to reach up and shake hands with the tank men.

The tank commanders and the gunners, André thought, were even wilder-looking creatures than the 'chutists.

The men seemed colossal, standing in their turrets before the radio antennae that wavered nervously, like an insect's feelers, with the sway of the tanks. Pushed-up goggles over helmets, and earphones, made drivers and gunners seem part of the weird contraptions.

"They are wonderful," André said. "I wish I could have seen them come ashore from the ships that brought them across the Channel."

Sergeant Weller frowned. "I don't think you'd have liked it, son. Only a few hours ago these men came off landin' craft that were bein' shot at by Nazis from every direction. These guys are just the lucky ones that didn't get hit."

The gathered villagers cheered, and the sound of their welcome rang out far up the road.

André was still looking for Victor. But Victor had not been seen that day.

André sauntered over to where the colonel had joined Dobie and the others in the window.

"Captain," André began. "Sir, about Victor—"

"I know," smiled the captain. "You wonder why he doesn't come back. I feel sure he'll be all right. If that car full of Nazi officers got through the roads from Paris to here, then I'm sure your friend Victor can find his way around. The Nazi officers said they drove straight through Caen, Carentan, and right through our lines, if you please—British *and* American. They actually got as far as the Jacquard farm without being detected."

The colonel spoke up. "As a matter of fact, I don't think the German staff in Paris knew how much country our airborne troops were covering. How could they? We had jammed their coastal radio and radar stations all the way to Cherbourg. And the French Resistance and our men cut telephone land lines. So it was impossible for the commanding German general here on the peninsula to communicate with Paris."

"Those Nazi prisoners," said Dobie, "told us they came up from Paris to find out what was really happening here. Hitler believed that our invasion was coming at Calais."

"He sure missed the boat," Weller said cheerfully.

The last of the squadron of tanks had gone by,

and the village people were returning to their homes. André went back to the farmyard. It was time for chores. He heard laughter coming from the barns, but by now he was used to soldier sounds.

First, he must see how badly the orchard and fields in the rear had been hit by the shelling. He went through the gate in the courtyard wall.

His jaw dropped. Many apple trees were down. Great smudged shell holes gaped between them. And the greatest hole yawned only a few feet away from the edge of the lane where his trumpet was buried.

He snatched up a shovel, and sighed in relief when the trumpet came up, green and smeared with damp earth, but unharmed. He nestled it comfortably under his arm and went to the barn door.

The cows had not lowed, and now he saw why. Balanced on stools beside the animals sat two lusty Americans. They were happily squirting streams into milk pails held correctly between their knees.

One of the soldiers looked up curiously.

At the sight of the horn under André's arm he cried, "Well, if it isn't Little Boy Blue, horn and all."

The second milker called, "These cows yours? We thought nobody was home. Sure seems good to milk an ole bossy again." He grinned. "I come from Iowa an' I sure miss milkin' time. Hope you don't mind. We're almost through here."

The men paused to admire André's trumpet, and tootle a few wild notes, before they helped him carry the pails to the springhouse. He filled a pitcher for Captain Dobie, and took it to the "staff room," as the old store was now called. The room was again filled with strange soldiers, some of them in bloody bandages.

The colonel was anxious to get away to his division command post.

"You stay right here, Dobie," he said, "and the sergeant and Slim as well. And hustle medics and replacement infantry forward, fast."

Slim appeared and announced that he had Weller's jeep ready to drive the colonel to his headquarters.

When Captain Dobie and André were alone, the captain smiled and sighed. "A fine mother I turned out to be," he said. "*When* did you eat something last?"

André grinned shyly. "When did *you* eat last, sir?"

Sergeant Weller's voice roared from the hallway, "Lunch coming up!"

A large loaded tray appeared through the door, followed by Weller's bulky body.

André looked at a heaped platter in the middle, and laughed. "So that is where our chickens went."

"Your father will be paid for these fowl," Dobie said. "So make up for the eating you haven't done today."

Weller was not as good a cook as his mother or Marie, André thought. But he was surprised that a tough sergeant could cook at all, and the meal was good.

When the sun sank red behind the trees, an evening hush settled, although soldiers from nearby bivouacs moved through the village restlessly.

Weller yawned. "I hope it stays quiet around here awhile," he said. "After last night we could do with a little snooze, eh, Captain?"

He had scarcely made this wish than André cried, "Listen!"

A distant sound of motors from the sky was drowned by the opening bark of an American antiaircraft battery close by.

Weller leaped to put out the lights.

"Might have known the Luftwaffe would wake up about now," he grumbled.

Captain Dobie's voice came out of the darkness. "I've been wondering why we haven't heard from them these last two days. Our air boys must have pretty thoroughly crippled them."

Ears were strained to follow the sounds.

"Must be several planes," Dobie said. "They seem to be dropping small bombs."

Weller, at the window, called, "Looks like a Fourth of July celebration."

Suddenly he shouted, *"We got one!"*

In the darkness, André listened to the wild whine of the falling Luftwaffe plane.

André reached Weller's side in time to see flames spring high above the dark treetops beyond the village.

"I didn't see any 'chute," Weller exclaimed.

"The pilot may have jumped before the fire lit up the sky," the captain replied.

The sudden flare of excitement was followed by an equally sudden lull except for the sound of soldiers' voices across the fields. The flack guns lapsed into silence.

Captain Dobie said, "Whew! Next time, André, you go down to the cellar. I forgot all about you for a minute."

Slim and a detail of men were sent off to look for the fallen Nazi plane, and also for the pilot.

"Better send out word to the French people around here to be on the lookout," Dobie added, "till we're sure about him."

When Slim and the men had been gone only a few minutes, Weller began to fidget restlessly.

"How about I just take a look-see down the road, Captain?" he suggested

Captain Dobie said okay, and Weller swept up a Tommy gun and went off into the night.

He had gone only a few yards when André caught up with him.

In a field, the last flames were flickering from the fallen Messerschmitt. A faint drizzle blurred the scene, but the figures of many soldiers were dimly silhouetted against the light.

"No good goin' over there," Weller said, after studying the scene a moment.

They had just begun to retrace their steps when Weller said, "Listen."

André had heard sounds too—a creaking and the clop, clop of hoofbeats.

Coming down the wet road a new, unpainted cart rattled into sight. Between the shafts clumped La Fumée. And, waving the reins behind the dashboard, stood Victor.

"André!" he shouted. "Where did you go?" He brushed at his enormous mustache nervously. "Well, never mind now. Get in. Get in. I'll drive you home."

André gulped with relief. Weller demanded, "Ask him how he got home."

André repeated the question in French, and Victor threw out his hands indignantly.

"How *should* I come?" he shouted. "By any open road those soldiers and tanks left for my use. Americans, Americans everywhere! Tanks! Guns! I have been halfway around the world to get here, it seems."

"But where did you find your cart? I thought it was blown up!" André cried.

Victor's eyebrows expressed more astonishment. "Where *would* I find it? Just where Jacquard said he would leave it, of course. Beyond his shop, among the holly trees."

When this was translated, Weller shook his head. "Well, climb in an' let's go home."

La Fumée, sensing the nearness of her own stable, started briskly.

When they had said good night to Victor, Weller yawned loudly.

André watched Weller, and laughed. "I'm pretty sleepy, myself," he admitted.

Ten minutes later he was in his mother's big bed, sprawled sound asleep.

CHAPTER ELEVEN

André and the Nazi Pilot

FALLING into bed, André's thoughts had turned to his family, but his worries were quickly drowned in sleep.

When he awoke, he ran downstairs to see what the sunrise had brought.

It had brought Victor.

André saw the old man—scrubbed pink and bristling—beside the guard at the door. With Victor was another of the village fathers—a farmer who had once been a schoolteacher. M. Blanc was a tall, square man, in a rough tweed suit.

"I am here," said Victor, speaking to both André and the guard—who did not understand a word—"about a matter which demands attention. It is the exasperating fact that an unexploded shell reposes in my—"

André cried, "Wait!" and hastily translated for the guard's benefit.

Victor remained standing, with open mouth. The guard shouted, and Slim came running. The captain was swiftly consulted, and a demolition squad was rounded up. This took only a few seconds, since disposing of unexploded shells was an ever-present problem.

On being questioned about where the "dud" was, Victor finished his sentence. "In my parlor, near the bay window."

At the last word, the demolition crew started running.

André asked, "But isn't Mme. Lescot frightened?"

"She does not even know it is there," Victor replied. "She has been off helping with some of the children since yesterday. I was obliged to prepare my own supper," he finished crossly.

Captain Dobie came to the door and gravely shook hands with the two Frenchmen. He eyed Victor curiously. After a moment's study of the old man, however, he decided that to order Victor to stay out of danger would be a waste of time.

It was M. Blanc who spoke.

"We came, sir," he said, "as spokesmen for the whole neighborhood. We wish to offer our services in any way you Americans consider helpful. We should also be grateful if you can tell us what to expect in the way of future danger to our community."

"I think," replied Captain Dobie, "you people have accepted all this destruction with fine, very brave spirit. The Maquis, as well as all you other French people, have helped the landing forces more than you will ever know. We Americans want you to realize that we are grateful. It could have been much worse for us."

M. Blanc put up a hand. "Please, m'sieur, it is our battle also. And the Maquis have told us that the Americans up beyond Ste. Mère are heroic."

The captain said his men had been wonderful. "But until we dispose of these Germans, we can't move forward into France beyond this peninsula."

"And the Canadians and British?" asked M. Blanc.

"They've successfully landed a lot of troops and tanks. They've penetrated to a considerable depth toward Caen, I hear."

"*Bon!*" Victor's head bobbed. "When you have disposed of these bothersome Nazis you speak of— you do what?"

Captain Dobie frowned. "We must throw a line of troops from these beaches straight across the neck of the peninsula to cut off German reinforcements from coming to the rescue of the enemy in Cherbourg."

"No doubt," frowned Victor, "the Nazis will respond by doing all the damage possible to our fine Cherbourg port."

"I'm afraid they will," agreed the captain. "When we take the port, our U. S. Army engineers will have to repair the docks quickly. We intend to bring in our main supplies for the liberation of the rest of France through Cherbourg when it is free."

"Capitaine Dobay," M. Blanc said, "I suppose no one knows how long the Germans will hold out."

"I'm afraid not," replied Captain Dobie.

There was a second shaking of hands, and Victor and M. Blanc left.

André's mind turned anxiously to the tale of heavy fighting which was moving toward St. Sauveur le Vicomte and his family there. He felt more cut off from them than ever, now that he knew they were surrounded by such desperate enemies.

"Has anybody found that German pilot yet?" he asked Captain Dobie.

"No sign of him," the captain replied. "Now, after breakfast, I have a job for Slim. And I think you and your dog could go along."

Half an hour later, André was telling a delighted Patchou, "They think it's safe now, for you to come out with me. But there's still a war on, so behave yourself."

The cows, he found, had again been milked by the American farmer-soldiers, and again most of

AT THE NORMANDY INVASION

the milk had vanished. The other barn chores had also been neatly done.

He heard soft sounds in the loft over the cow barn, and crept up the stairs to investigate.

A dozen or more soldiers from the night patrol were sleeping heavily in the sweet hay. Full of good Gagnon milk, André thought with pleasure.

He tiptoed down the stairs and, freeing Patchou from his fastening, answered Slim's impatient halloo.

"Gotta find a commissary dump somewhere down the road," Slim explained. "Weller says it cain't be far. Them 90th Division cooks told him about it."

After his long imprisonment, Patchou was blissfully happy. He ran rings around Slim and André. He found excitement in every newly blasted hole in the mossy walls, and inviting scents everywhere.

Slim marched rapidly along for nearly half a mile, with André keeping up at a trot. Then Slim said, "Best we begin to ask questions now. Who, 'round here, knows everything?"

André pointed to a house ahead. "That's M. Valjean's home there. He's the cobbler. He will know."

M. Valjean listened eagerly to André's query. Did he know where there was an American food dump headquarters near by?

"Ah-h, *oui, oui, certainement,*" the cobbler responded enthusiastically, and gave detailed directions in a flood of rapid French.

André said, "I know where it is." He added, *"Merci,"* to M. Valjean.

"You sure?" Slim frowned. "Sounded as if it must be on the Russian border, what-all I could make of it."

"I am sure, Slim," André replied. "It is my own schoolhouse."

Slim's rapidly swinging long legs kept André at an almost breathless canter. Because their minds were silently busy, they did not hear the word, *"Kamerad,"* when it was first spoken.

But Slim's reaction to something out of key stopped him short, .45 in hand.

André was pushed back before the second, louder, *"Kamerad"* gave him warning.

CHAPTER TWELVE

Slim and the Trumpet

SLIM leaned forward intently, staring at a thicket to one side. "Who're you? Come out—hands up!" he shouted. "Get back, kid."

A voice said, "It is not necessary. I vish to giff myself up—villingly."

A young German airman stepped from behind the litter of broken cherry branches.

"Where'd you come from?" Slim demanded. "Keep those hands on your head."

"I know who he is," André cried. Then, to the stranger, "You're the pilot who jumped from the Messerschmitt, aren't you?"

The German nodded. "I vish to make no trouble. Please take my gun—a Luger only, in the holster."

Slim snapped out the pistol. "Listen," he demanded, "what gives here?"

The German said, "I haf vanted to giff up a long time now. I am glad you haff come."

"Well," Slim shrugged, "maybe you can explain that to the captain. Come on. March ahead of me to that schoolhouse yonder."

When they reached the food dump, the prisoner was put under guard. Meanwhile Slim carried out the captain's orders for food supplies. Slim pointed to the stacked cartons he had piled in the corner of the schoolhouse. "See nobody lays a hand on that. A jeep'll be over to pick it up within an hour," he told the commissary sergeant. He also asked for an extra guard to accompany them back to the captain. "He says he wants to give hisself up," Slim said, "but how do we know he's on the level?"

Drawing his own gun, Slim added to André, as he led the way, "Wouldn't our flack gunners like to get a look at this Luftwaffe fellow?"

The prisoner smiled wryly. "Your flack gunners already haff seen me," he said. "That is vhy I am here."

On their return, Captain Dobie greeted the German with surprising enthusiasm. "I am delighted to see you," he said. "You had us worried."

"I vas vorried myself, sir," the pilot replied.

A few minutes later the prisoner was dispatched to an interrogation center by jeep, with Weller and a guard.

Captain Dobie suggested that André find M. Blanc and tell him that the village could forget about that particular German pilot. "Glad to have *him* off my mind," the captain added.

André found M. Blanc consulting with Victor near the end of the village and gave them the captain's good news.

En route home through the fields, André found an almost undamaged yellow parachute. "How beautiful Marie will be in a dress of yellow silk!" he thought. And he folded it carefully, tucking the bulky load under his arm.

That evening, after supper, André took his trumpet into the kitchen. He gathered cleaning rags and polish, and rubbed and cleaned the brass of the horn. When the tubes had been cleared and the metal gleamed, he piped a little trill of lonely notes.

They made him feel no better, and he tried a Normandy dance tune.

He heard the clump of feet behind him and Slim's voice. "Holy cow! *Where* did you get that horn?"

André put the trumpet down shyly. Slim picked it up carefully and rubbed the mouthpiece with his sleeve.

"Can you play a trumpet?" André asked curiously.

"Waal . . . I used to play some in the school

band in Pecos, Texas. Matter of fact, I was pretty good. Shall I give 'er a try?"

André jumped when a ringing peal of notes rose from the brass to the rafters. The notes slid down the scale, and Slim broke loudly into "Turkey in the Straw."

Weller's bellow rose even above the music's vibrations. "Stop that racket!" Slim guiltily took the horn from his lips. The sergeant shouted, "Captain's on the phone to headquarters."

"Tell you what, André," Slim whispered. "Suppose we go try this out somewhere?"

For the next hour, in the dimly lit springhouse, André enjoyed himself more than he had for weeks. And when Slim said, "Time for bed now," André had learned half of Slim's pet song, which was something about Texas.

Next morning, André found that a thick fog, almost a drizzle, hung over the treetops. The soft gray mist hid the harsh destruction of the landscape.

André went out to find Raoul at work patching the Coty roof. "Just help me with this thatch, will you?" Raoul called.

André gladly climbed up the old ladder with an armful of straw while Raoul chattered.

But a moment later he stopped listening to Raoul's talk. Somewhere in the fog, he had detected the uncertain throbbing of a plane's engine.

André had learned half of Slim's pet song

He sat still to follow the sound. The plane was flying in wide circles, steadily coming in lower.

In a drift of the mist, André caught a glimpse of the markings—a white star.

"He's in trouble, Raoul. That's an American plane," André cried.

"How could he be in trouble?" Raoul objected. "He's still in the sky, is he not?"

But listening closely, he too, heard the engine sputter. "That engine needs repairs!" he declared disapprovingly.

Hastily, André shouted, "DUCK!"

Their heads went down as the plane's wings, trailing wisps of fog, swept close overhead. André had just time to make out a high-wing monoplane with patches and holes in its fabric covering.

The plane banked, sailed over a field behind the Coty house, and was set down expertly.

André was already scrambling down the ladder.

He pelted across the meadow with no thought of danger. Racing toward the plane, he thought only that the pilot might be hurt. Through the plexiglass enclosure of the little ship, André saw a blond young fellow, in an odd, peaked cap.

At the sound of pounding footsteps, the pilot whirled, an automatic suddenly in his hand and pointed at André.

CHAPTER THIRTEEN

The War from the Air

ANDRÉ was so surprised that he stammered, in English, "D—don't fire!"

The flyer's hand dropped. *"Parlez-vous* English?" he faltered, frowning.

André's suspicions leaped up. Dirty brown coveralls, the strange cap, the German-looking, tow-colored hair. And the plane. André had never seen one like it, and the star insigne could be a Nazi fake.

André stood his ground, some distance away. When the pilot flung open the side door and jumped out, André stepped back.

In a swift glance over his shoulder, André saw Raoul reach the bottom of the ladder. He shouted, "Run get Slim, Raoul. And tell the captain."

"For the love of Mike, kid, what gives with you? You think I'm a German?" the pilot demanded.

"You could be," André retorted.

"Holy mackerel!" the pilot laughed. "That's what I thought you were, at first. I didn't even see you were a kid when I pulled the gun. Forget it."

"Well," André admitted after a moment, "you do talk like an American."

"How come?"

André laughed uncertainly. "Germans don't say 'How come,' for one thing," he stated. "But what *are* you doing here? It looks as though you were lost."

"Lost is right—and out of fuel, too," the pilot replied with angry disgust. "Now I've got to find more gas and get over to Utah Beach in a hurry. Where am I, anyway?"

"You are about four miles from the nearest invasion beach," André said. "But I'm not sure of the different names you Americans have given them. Someone will be here soon. Captain Dobie can't come himself, he has a broken leg."

"Is this Dobie's command?" the flyer exclaimed. "Well, I'm in a hurry. Cripes! I can't keep the general waiting. He'll give me hoop-la for navigating myself into this mess—fog or no fog. Here's somebody now."

It was Slim, at a gallop, followed by two armed guards. They fell in on each side of the pilot.

Slim took a quick look at the flyer and the plane, and asked, "What outfit *you* with?"

"Army Liaison Squadron, Lieutenant Bill Carson," replied the pilot. "You with the 82nd Airborne?"

Slim nodded and asked sharply, "Now, what's up here? Don't you guys use landin' strips any more?"

"Don't pile it on, buddy," Carson said. "I'm in bad enough already. I got myself lost good, in this weather. And this kid here thought I was a German—"

Slim turned sternly to André. "You can overdo this takin' prisoners without consultin' us, you know, son," he muttered coldly.

He explained to the pilot, more mildly, "This André and an old Frenchman helped catch a car full of Nazi officers once. But once is enough."

The lieutenant stared at André. "Say," he exclaimed, "are you the French kid I heard about? Trapped those German staff officers? I bet my general'd like to shake hands with you. He's the one who questioned them."

Slim put on his best corporal's manner. "Best we get back to your business here, Lieutenant. How are you going to wangle your jalopy out of this corner, now you got her wedged in so good?"

The pilot shrugged. "Get me some gas, and I'll fly out okay. Might have to wait till the fog lifts a little."

Slim pondered a moment. "Listen, André. You think we could squeeze a little more gas out of that pump of your dad's? Take us an hour or more to waylay a U. S. truck carryin' gas."

André smiled. "We've been telling everyone the pump was empty, but we have a little left in case of—you know—"

Carson gave a yelp. "I know—emergency, you mean. Well, boys, I'm the worst emergency you'll ever meet."

Slim ordered one of his men to guard the plane. At a frown from the guard, Raoul, who had been standing close by, stalked off.

At the house Slim went in to report to the captain and came back with word that Dobie had telephoned the general waiting at Utah Beach.

The general had sent a message to Carson: "What did that idiot mean by getting stuck in a blasted cow pasture? And tell him to get out of there in a blasted hurry, or I'll have his blasted . . ." and so forth.

Carson smiled wanly. "That's my general," he said.

Slim went back to duty, and André and the pilot refilled the plane's tank from the cans they had brought from the Gagnon pump.

Carson took a dismal look at the gray-blanketed landscape. With André's help, he rolled the machine around so that it headed away from the hedge. "Want to get in while I taxi her into position?" Carson asked.

"You are permitted—?" André cried.

Carson laughed. "Of course I'm not permitted —but what's the difference? Climb in."

André clambered into the seat beside the pilot's. Carson turned a switch, adjusted the throttle, swung the propeller, and the engine started promptly. "Now, fasten that seat belt and hold on, this field's bumpy."

With a surge of power, the plane began to move. Skillfully the pilot ruddered a jolting course around the potholes and stumps, to the far corner of the meadow. "Need all the run I can get for the take-off," he explained.

Faced around for a diagonal course, he throttled the engine. "Gosh, I think the fog is beginning to break," he cried.

He leaned out to observe the wind direction which already was beginning to ruffle the tops of the trees.

"I'd feel better if I knew this country," he said. "You know it like your own hand, I suppose?"

André said he did, and the pilot stared down at him thoughtfully.

"Say," Carson broke out again. "How about you coming along for the ride, and point out landmarks for me?"

André's eyes lit up. "But—" he began.

"You seen the Invasion beaches yet? I'll show them to you," he offered.

Before André could gather his wits, Carson exclaimed, "There's a patch of blue sky! We better grab this chance. Hang on. Here we go!" And he pushed open the throttle.

André felt the engine quicken and then the forward jolt as the brakes were released.

Smoothly, the little ship lifted after the short run. Banking sharply, it swept toward the far rim of trees and, with inches to spare, skimmed over them.

The mist was breaking up, revealing open vistas. As the plane rose, the houses and fields below shrank away swiftly.

The pilot said, "Keep a close watch for low-flying bombers. They're all over the place today, cleaning out isolated German pockets."

Almost at once they were over the marshes.

"That's our road to the sea." André pointed.

The mists broke away sharply over the Channel. André gasped.

A staggering panorama had been unveiled. Pigmy files of marching troops, pigmy tanks and trucks crawled up the sea road in an endless procession. Oceanward, beyond the shore bluff and wreck-strewn beach, lay a sight which André could scarcely take in. Hundreds of ships extended as far as he could see across the gray waves. Over the ships, huge balloons lolled and bobbed and tugged at their anchors. Destroyers and landing craft darted between the shore and a line of hundreds of transports.

André could make out a fleet of planes heading toward Cherbourg to the north. And from that direction, the dull thud of bombs rolled back on the wet air.

"It is grand," he managed to say breathlessly. "But—" he hesitated, and added slowly, "it is terrible for the French people. So many guns and bombs pointed at us."

Carson glanced down at him. "They are pointed at the Germans," he corrected André. "Don't forget that we're trying not to hurt France more than necessary."

"*Oui,* I know," André said. "But sir, I did not know there were so many ships and guns in the whole world."

"Well," said Carson, "take a good look while you've got the chance. I've got my bearings now."

André studied the beach below. In the shallow

water, wrecked landing craft swung uselessly, half-awash. On the sea's edge lay tanks which had reached shore only to be shelled into wreckage. Savage battles had turned the sands into a disorder of blasted, blackened gun pits and machine-gun nests.

Twice, while Carson circled, André saw him fiddling with the radio. Then he spoke into the hand microphone, and listened for a few moments.

"Got 'em at last," he said. "They say we've got

to hold off awhile longer. Some Luftwaffe guy got through last night and bombed the strip. They're just finishing repairs. See them down there?"

André looked directly down. Tiny men laying strips of steel mesh moved in groups, like ants. Bulldozers swept along one side. And between the airstrip and the sea, supplies were piling up steadily into mountains.

Carson grinned. "I'll bet that's my general pacing up and down in front of that big tent." A second later, he said, "As long as we can't get down right away, how about we take a look at the English and Canadian beachheads?"

He swung alongshore and headed eastward.

Carson pointed out the little city of Carentan. There was a rattle of machine guns below, and the pilot threw the plane into a series of violent turns. Noises like angry wasps streaked past their ears.

André swayed dizzily.

"Oh-oh! What am I doing in here?" Carson yelled. "That's the way I get holes in my ship." He pointed out new tears in the fabric. As they zoomed away, he explained, "That was a Nazi machine gun. There are still German troops and guns between Utah and Omaha Beaches and the British beachheads."

The plane climbed steadily away, and André relaxed.

The fury of Omaha and the British beaches was very like that which he had seen at Utah.

Unconsciously, André shuddered. Far to the right, under a pall of smoke and the flickering of explosions, lay a city being pounded to rubble.

"That must be Caen," André murmured. "My mother was born in Caen." Then, after a moment, "The houses, the farms, the cows and the horses . . . the people . . ." he counted sadly.

Carson sat thoughtfully quiet. He swung the ship in a wide circle for the return.

"Don't think about it, kid," he said presently. "Just remember the big German guns that aren't there any more."

André replied slowly, "I don't think we really knew the Liberation would be as bad as this. We will be glad when it is over."

Suddenly the pilot jammed his control stick forward. The plane nosed into a violent dive. "Hang on! Fighters overhead. Up there!" he shouted.

André's head had jerked back. In his range of vision, a formation of six Thunderbolts with white stars roared past.

"Wow!" Carson gasped, and pulled the ship level.

"They're after a bridge," he yelled.

André watched plane after plane go into a dive and the bombs leave the racks to arc downward.

In the successive rain of bombs a black, flame-flecked cloud shot skyward.

"They have hit it!" André cried jubilantly.

The Thunderbolts zoomed upward out of the haze, reformed, and disappeared toward England.

Some time later, Carson talked once more into the radio. "It's okay. They say to come in now. The runway's ready," he announced.

He throttled back. "Well, now you know what the beaches are like," he sighed. There was a smooth descent, Carson slid in over the steel mesh and brought the machine to a stop beside a group of officers.

He snapped open his own seat belt and André's. "Oh-oh!" Carson gasped. "I'd better try to explain *you*."

André looked across at a glistening, brilliant red face that belonged to a bulky man in a sweat-stained uniform.

"It's the general," Carson whispered. He pushed the door open and saluted.

He spoke more rapidly than usual. "This is the French boy, sir, who helped catch the Nazi brass from Paris."

The general seemed to be caught between fury and curiosity.

"Is it!" he sputtered at last. "And *what's* he doing in an army plane?"

"Well, sir—" Carson blinked. "I needed—"

"Oh, never mind," boomed the general explosively. "He's here now, and I want to shake hands with him. Come on, boy."

André leaped down from the plane, and his hand disappeared in the general's bear clutch.

"Glad to thank you personally—" roared the huge man gruffly.

He mopped his neck. "Want to tell you—what's your name again? André Gunion? Can't get these foreign names. Rotten at languages, but I can judge people. Where's that old fellow—friend of yours—Vilmer, was it?—who shot the tires off the Nazis?"

André had tried to speak several times. Now, he said loudly, "Victor—Lescot."

"Lescot? Lescot? That means green vegetable, doesn't it?" barked the general. "No? Well, never mind. Congratulate him for me. Found out a lot from those Nazi colonels, we did. Tell you what. We expect the biggest generals we got, here on this bridgehead in a couple of days—Eisenhower, Marshall, Arnold. They'll be glad to know how you French kids have helped."

He paused for breath. "Well, got to get going. Lieutenant!"

Carson emerged from inspecting the bullet holes in the plane, again chattering rapidly. "How are we going to get this boy home, sir? He can't walk. It's too far."

The general snorted. "Send him in a jeep, of course—with some new orders for Captain Dobie."

An iron-faced sergeant appeared and saluted.

"Oh, there you are, Streukoff," shouted the general. "Take this boy to Captain Dobie. Boy knows where his command post is, over there somewhere." He jerked a large thumb toward inland Normandy.

At the plane, he called back, "And mind you get a receipt for him."

Carson called to André, "We had fun, eh? Be seeing you," and opened the throttle.

Half an hour later, a jeep bearing André in the front seat, rocketed around a line of trucks and soldiers into André's own village.

He had been busy for some minutes thinking how he was to explain his trip to Captain Dobie.

As the jeep rolled down the village street André saw that something unusual had happened. The neighbors were running toward a little gathering of people.

His eyes raced over them and stopped.

In front of the parish house, worn, gray with fatigue, his clothes dusty and torn, loomed a tall old man.

André's heart stood still.

"Father Duprey!" he shouted.

CHAPTER FOURTEEN

Father Duprey's Story

M Y DEAR boy!" Father Duprey held out his arms.

André cleared the space to the parsonage steps as though shot from the jeep.

"Did my mother come—my father—Marie?" he cried.

He looked up at the priest's long, bony face, lined with weariness, and halted. The old man's embrace was kind, but André knew at once that the news he brought was not good. His expression held too much sadness.

"The father needs rest," someone in the crowd of neighbors called out. And Anna, the parsonage housekeeper, bustled from the door.

"Come in, come in, André," she called anxiously. "And bring in the father. I will give you tea. And *then* you may talk."

"My dear boy!" Father Duprey held out his arms

"I must tell you, André," Father Duprey said, "my news of your family is not too bad. So do not be anxious. However, I do not know where all of them are now. But come into the house."

After tea was served, the old man sighed deeply. "Now, André," he said, "to relieve your anxiety as well as I can.

"To begin. The hospital where we left your mother is small. And it is well outside the town of St. Sauveur le Vicomte—in the country, really. The doctors there are good. Your father, Marie, and I waited for some time to get a report from them about your mother.

"At about ten-thirty o'clock, Monday night— that was June 5th—one of the doctors came to tell us that Mme. Gagnon needed only the right medicine and a week or two to get well. That is good news, eh?"

André sighed. "Yes, very good."

"Ah! another thing." The priest held up a thin finger. "The Maquis met us exactly on time, at the rendezvous not far from the hospital. And your brave English flyer—Ronald Pitt—ran for it. What a sight! Two of the roughest looking of our Maquis and a nun, racing toward a near-by building. But—well, they got away safely. That *was* good, no?"

"Wonderful," André murmured.

"Well, then. At about eleven-thirty that night,

your father and I stood at the hospital door. We were to start back home, and Marie was to stay with your mother. We heard bombing all around us. Your father said, 'The bombing is getting bad.'

"Just as he said that, we heard loud shouting in German, and Nazis began pouring out of their camp onto the roads.

"A minute later there was the sound of motorcycles and cars shrieking in the streets, and heavy antiaircraft fire.

"Someone cried out, 'The Invasion has begun! *Parachutists are landing all around Ste. Mère!'*

"Your father felt that his duty was to remain with Mme. Gagnon. I, that my duty was to hasten home. And I promised to look after you, André."

The old man smiled wryly. "I did not have much chance to do that, did I?

"In the midst of it, Marie appeared. She was with Leon Duplis, a Maquis I know well.

"She said, 'Father, the Maquis here need women to help with the villagers. Please do not forbid me to go. In the hospital, Mother is in good hands.' "

"Your father agreed, but not willingly. In another minute Marie and Leon were on a motorcycle and out of sight."

"But how did you get home, father? It has been five days," asked André.

The priest replied, "It was necessary to follow the loneliest roads through the confusion. One did not know where the shells or the snipers' bullets would strike.

"I slept well enough under hedges," the priest continued. "I was very kindly given food by many villagers. Sometimes I took refuge in a church or house. At times I was able to help with the wounded and ill. And sometimes I stopped to comfort the children."

Father Duprey rose and put a kindly hand on André's shoulder. "I am glad that you were spared, son. Go home now, and do not worry. Even about Marie. The Gagnons are a family that for two hundred years has not been easily crushed."

André went slowly down the parsonage steps. . . . On the first night of the invasion his parents had been safe. But that was four days ago, he thought.

A loud shout stopped him. Streukoff beckoned from the jeep. "Hey, kid! Say, I gotta deliver you and get a receipt from Captain Dobie. Git in."

André looked shocked. "The general was joking, wasn't he? I can walk the short distance home. I'm sorry I kept you waiting so long."

"Oh, that's all right. I needed the rest," grinned Streukoff. "But I'm getting that receipt, boy. A general never forgets."

Captain Dobie looked up from his desk irritably when Streukoff entered the room and saluted. André followed well in the rear.

"Yes?" Dobie snapped.

After hearing the general's request, he barked, "You want *what*? You brought André home? From *where!*"

At one side, Weller muttered, "I should 'a' known better. I should 'a' known better."

The captain scribbled out a receipt for Streukoff and signed it. He then registered his feelings by banging weights down on all the papers on his desk.

"I never even *missed* him," he said through closed lips.

The telephone jangled, and André saw Weller turn to Captain Dobie excitedly.

"It's the colonel," Weller shouted. "We're movin' this command post up to the other side of Ste. Mère! The 9th division is almost set to help us on a big push."

Weller turned his eyes slowly on André.

CHAPTER FIFTEEN

Battle for St. Sauveur

THE idea of Captain Dobie's staff going away came as a shock to André.

"B-but—" he stammered.

Captain Dobie and Weller consulted maps and papers. At last, the captain sat back and lit a cigarette.

"You've seen Father Duprey? What did he have to tell you?" he inquired mildly.

"Not very good news, sir," André replied. "But nothing especially bad . . . I wish my family could get home," he said irritably.

Captain Dobie cocked an eyebrow.

"I wish they could, too," he said. "And, as long as I am responsible here, maybe you'd like to tell me why you went off with that pilot in his plane."

At this unexpected shift, André flushed.

"You did not tell me not to, sir," he said shyly.

"I did not tell you not to ride an elephant to Afghanistan, either," the captain retorted. "How could I know you had any intention of flying over the enemy?"

"I did not know it myself." André could not help smiling. "It just happened."

"Well, you're lucky to be back. I don't suppose

it really matters if I turn gray worrying about you," said the captain.

A bark from Patchou in the kitchen gave André an excuse to bolt away.

Although Captain Dobie's colonel had ordered the post moved closer to the fighting, the change would not come until other units were in position.

During the next couple of days André's mind turned more and more toward St. Sauveur. If he could only go forward with Dobie and Weller and Slim, to be near when that town was liberated. Other French children were in the battle zone. And, after all, he had been under fire himself.

St. Sauveur, Weller explained, was directly in the path of the Americans who were hammering through to the coast to keep the Germans from sending help to the fortress at Cherbourg. The 9th Division and their own 82nd Airborne were working together in this drive for the showdown.

Weller came home from an errand to the beach on Tuesday, the 13th, whistling gaily, off key.

"Good news?" André asked.

Weller replied, "Tops. We wiped the Nazis out of that gap between Utah and Omaha beachheads. Now we can roll! And boy! You ought to see our new Utah airstrip. Planes goin' to London out of there—like ferries—with the wounded."

Captain Dobie, talking to his colonel on the phone, hung up, looking cheerful.

"The towns along the Merderet River seem to be pretty well mopped up," he reported. "We hold the bridges. So the way to the Douve River's clear now."

Later that day Weller made a fast trip to the new command post. He came back to report that a small stone farm building near a crossroads north of Pont l'Abbé had been found for Captain Dobie.

"We got a pair of new lieutenants takin' the places of a couple that got wounded," Weller said. "Good fighters, these replacements, Schoenfargle an' Ouvarski."

André grew more silent as the captain's leaving day drew near.

St. Sauveur was to André a pretty little town where his family were. As each day went by he felt more anxious about his mother. And finally he decided he must follow Dobie and look for her.

On the last evening, Captain Dobie said, "I'm leaving Slim here for a few days, on orders, André. He'll be in touch with me, so send us word if anything is wrong."

Weller echoed, "Yeah. You do that, kid, and you just tend to the cows, and mind what Father Duprey says."

André was up and the house astir before sunrise next morning.

Maps, papers, and duffle were stacked waiting

in the hallway when Slim appeared at the door and announced, "Jeep's ready, Captain."

This was the bad moment for André.

Dobie hobbled out to the jeep and Weller followed. Several of the neighbors, including Father Duprey and Victor, had come to say good-by.

Patchou kept up a nervous barking, shocked by the departure of friends, until André put an arm around him.

Over the noisy complaint of the jeep's motor, Captain Dobie thanked all those gathered there for their help. And he asked that thanks be given to the Gagnons.

"I'll see you all again," he smiled, clutching at his seat as the jeep leaped forward.

And up to the overhanging chestnut trees rang cries of *"Vive l'Amérique!"* and *"Vive le Capitaine Dobay!"*

The last André heard was Weller's voice, bellowing, "Vive la Frenchmen!"

The silence of the house, as the sun slid up over the trees, was numbing.

Mme. Lescot arrived to break this up, equipped with an armload of cleaning things.

"This place resembles a pigsty," she announced. "Mme. Gagnon must not see such a mess. Please cause yourself to be absent."

Slim hurriedly remembered a job to be done.

André pushed Patchou hastily out of doors and went to milk the cows.

He had just put the milk to cool when Mme. Lescot hailed him from the kitchen door. "Breakfast!" she called.

When Slim and André drew up to the table, Mme. Lescot produced a breakfast of army supplies she had found on a shelf.

"It is not my business," she said shortly, "to complain about God's behavior. But I cannot help believing He has encouraged the American Army to habits of extravagance. Do you leave good food behind, everywhere you go?"

When this was translated into English, Slim laughed.

"No, ma'am!" he said emphatically. "This army eats everything it lays its hands on. Weller's just repayin' the Gagnons for the use of their house, I guess."

After breakfast, Slim called for André and the trumpet. Fitted in between his duties, Slim gave André more lessons in American tunes. The old house trembled under the blasts.

In the midst of one of Slim's Texas songs, an ambulance full of wounded from the fighting at St. Sauveur drew up and stopped.

The driver had a message about Captain Dobie.

"Cap'n's got himself shot in the shoulder," he reported.

André and Slim froze.

The driver added, as he started on, "Couldn't get him to come away and be evacuated home with these other guys."

"What's Weller doin' lettin' the skipper get shot!" Slim exclaimed. "Best I get up there quick, now."

André had decided to "get up there," too.

He could surely get far enough to trace Marie, and perhaps find some clue to where his father and mother were.

Late that evening of D-day plus nine, Weller returned to pick up Slim.

"Come on, Corporal," he shouted. "The cap'n needs you.

"Looks like we'll take St. Sauveur in a couple of days," he told André. "Then, as soon's we cut through to the coast, the big push up to Cherbourg starts off. Won't be long now . . . Take care y'self, kid."

The two waved from the jeep. "Be seein' you," they called.

André answered, *"Oui*—yes. I think so. Soon."

Because of his own plans, Slim's departure did not leave André quite so lonely as he might have been.

The question of *how* to get near St. Sauveur was the problem. André thought he might ask some pleasant-looking officer for a lift. He might—

In the end it was Victor who solved things very simply.

The Lescots' married daughter's home had been burned out. She had just sent word that she was at a farm near Picauville, a hamlet just outside Pont l'Abbé. The message begged her father to come, please, and get her.

On the morning after Slim's departure, Victor arrived at the Gagnons' door with La Fumée and the cart. He explained his journey to André.

"But," André cried, "I must go with you, Victor. You cannot speak English any better than you did when we went to Jacquard's."

"That is true enough," Victor admitted.

"Good. I go. I translate when soldiers try to stop you," André announced.

"It is an idea," Victor agreed.

"Well, then?" André cried.

"The cows," Victor chided.

André paused. "Raoul?" he suggested. "Do you think he would milk them?"

"Most certainly. And steal the milk, equally certainly," Victor said.

"I'll ask him," André decided. "Wait, *please.*"

"I will wait."

Victor sat impatiently in the cart and polished his glasses while André raced across the field.

Ten minutes later André was back. Raoul had agreed. And La Fumée was plodding steadily toward Ste. Mère and the clatter and shriek of gunfire. Crouching under a blanket at André's feet lay Patchou.

The Gagnon house stood silently empty for the first time in weeks.

About noon a black motorcycle rolled to a stop beside the Gagnon pump. Marie, in dark slacks and a man's cap similar to the driver's, dismounted.

"The house looks empty, Leon," she said, alarm in her voice.

She pushed open the door and called, "André." There was no answer as she entered the empty hallway.

Hurriedly, she ran through the house in a panic, and returned to the door.

"He isn't here, Leon," she cried. "The house is empty. Even Patchou is gone."

Leon looked at her calmly. "Perhaps you are not the only adventurous one in the family," he laughed.

Aghast at the thought of André wandering who knows where, Marie paused.

"I did hope he had a letter from Maman telling us where the hospital has moved to. And now I don't even know what has happened to André," she cried.

She looked wildly around the village.

Darting between passing trucks she came to the Lescot kitchen. A few minutes later she returned to Leon, breathless.

"André has gone off toward St. Sauveur with Victor," she explained. "Perhaps we can catch up with them on the road to Pont l'Abbé. We must hurry."

The black motorcycle shot off in the direction of Ste. Mère.

CHAPTER SIXTEEN

André into the Fighting

ANDRÉ'S trip with Victor was unexpectedly easy at the beginning.

When they passed through Ste. Mère, the town seemed almost quiet, although the litter and destruction on all sides were heartbreaking.

Beyond the town, the roads were clogged.

Victor was not challenged as they wove through marching troops and rolling equipment.

"That looks very unpleasant ahead of us," Victor stated disapprovingly, when they had crossed the Merderet River bridge.

Shell bursts, dust and smoke hung over the once orderly fields and patches of woods. Noises burst out loudly behind clumps of trees and died away.

Presently, Victor announced: "We proceed but a short distance farther along this road. At an oak tree ahead we turn left to the village where my daughter is."

It was then that André put forward his own plans. He watched Victor's look of shocked surprise anxiously. Suppose Victor would not let him go?

"But," Victor said, "you know I cannot accompany you into St. Sauveur now. Surely you comprehend that!"

André said firmly, "I did not expect it, Victor. I go on with Patchou only. Captain Dobie is near here, so I won't be alone."

Even as André said this, he began to doubt whether Captain Dobie would welcome him. He also began to wonder whether he could find the captain's new post.

As he and Victor drew nearer St. Sauveur, André began to notice that the sound of firing came from many directions. He turned his eyes from north to south and counted several rising pillars of smoke. Sometimes the ground shuddered and rocked the cart.

"It will not be easy to enter the city," he thought.

But after he and Victor had talked a minute, Victor agreed to let him go.

"However, you must use good sense," Victor said, as André climbed down from the cart. "Do not approach a single German, even if he looks kindly. You must recall that not all Nazis are like our Papa Schmidt."

After this good advice, he added, "You are quite right to seek your mother. I shall no doubt get along without you well enough."

With this, he clacked the reins and drove off.

André and Patchou skirted the jumbled rubble that had once been the village of Pont l'Abbé. They continued on through bypaths and across fields.

"If you stay close to me, you may walk," André told Patchou. Patchou trotted along obediently, his trembling shoulder pressed tightly against André's leg.

André looked at the skyline ahead. As he stared, new blazes broke out. Billowing smoke hung over St. Sauveur beyond the hills. After a moment he realized that the city was being bombarded by big guns.

"We may as well get as close to Maman as we can," he murmured. "Come along, Patchou." He could see a file of soldiers, hugging the roadside and straggling toward the city.

He led Patchou into a cowpath and they trudged on.

Twice André pulled Patchou down into a ditch as rifle and machine gun fire broke out in near-by villages.

After the second dive into a ditch, André sat

[*141*]

thoughtfully silent. It would be better to go back, he knew. But then he thought of his empty house—

"Come on, Patchou," he whispered. "When we get across the main road to St. Sauveur, just over there, we will try to find somebody to tell us how to find Maman in the hospital."

They scurried across the tree-lined highway.

Where they crossed, the road seemed deserted. André could not see far in any direction. Back in the fields a stone barn stood among shredded trees below a hill. A château stood on the hilltop, almost hidden by trees.

Just as André looked up, a shell arched down from the sky a hundred yards away.

Before André could grab Patchou's collar the explosion showered them both with stones and mud.

André reached wildly for Patchou and ran head-long with him into the field toward the nearest building he could see—the stone barn.

The blast of another shell threw André onto his face in a hail of debris. And Patchou twisted with a wild jerk and broke away.

André leaped to his feet, shrieking, "Patchou! Patchou!"

But Patchou had disappeared! And while André called wildly, another voice shouted, "Here, kid! Come here! The barn! Run, kid—*run!*"

The scream of another "88" from the sky brought André to his senses.

He saw a figure in the half-open door of the barn waving to him frantically.

André raced up to the entrance and threw himself into the arms of the tall soldier who had called. The door banged shut and the bolt was shot. Immediately a patter of machine-gun bullets rattled against the broad iron hinges. The hail of bullets whined and thudded steadily.

Another voice in the barn shouted angrily, "*Where* are the reinforcements, Lieutenant Ouvarski? Our ammo isn't going to hold out much longer."

The strong arms that had pulled André in set him on his feet, and he caught a glimpse of a lieutenant's shoulder bars.

The lieutenant said gently, "It's all right, boy. But what were you doing in the battle area?"

André could only gasp for breath. After a moment he stammered, "I—I didn't know I was so close to the line. Patchou? Can I get him soon?"

The light, from broken places in the roof high overhead, was dim. André caught glimpses of shadowy faces stationed at windows and small breaks in the walls. Rifles cracked, and a bazooka at a far window flamed.

"We're in a German trap," the lieutenant explained to André hastily. "I sent out for help. I hope it comes. You get over in that manger, kid, and keep down."

Then the lieutenant turned to shout orders and warnings to his men. "Don't show yourself above that window again, Donovan! You *want* to get hit?"

"Two Heinies edgin' around that wall," screamed an unseen rifleman. "Watch it, Lieutenant!"

After a shattering fusilade of machine-gun fire against the old stone walls, a sudden silence fell. And outside, a German voice called, "Do you giff up, or do we take you, vun by vun?"

Silence fell again. And then the bark of the lieutenant's automatic. Six rapid shots.

"There's your answer, Fritzie boy!" Lieutenant Ouvarski growled.

The voice outside did not speak again. The lieutenant wiped his face on the sleeve of his shirt.

André thought, "I hope my mother and father and Marie are in a deep stone cellar." Then suddenly he was too tired to remember why he was there.

He did not even hear the corporal say, "What does old Dobie think he's doin' about those reinforcements he promised? Sendin' 'em by way of Alaska?"

CHAPTER SEVENTEEN

Patchou on the Battlefield

A FEW minutes after André left Victor, Captain Dobie, Weller, their colonel, and his aide were poring over a map. They were hidden under trees, a mile and a half from the stone barn.

They looked up every moment or two toward St. Sauveur.

"Things are going along fine," the colonel said. "The engineers have got a rubber pontoon bridge over the Douve River, and troops are crossing there already. They'll have a steel one over the river for the tanks to cross, in an hour or two."

Dobie nodded. "How soon do you think we'll be sending our first patrols into St. Sauveur?" he asked.

"By sunset," the colonel said. "As soon as the 9th gets the rest of these towns around here cleaned up, we'll send our fellows through. How are those new lieutenants I sent you, Dobie?"

Captain Dobie grinned. "Schoenfargle took forty-seven prisoners yesterday. And Ouvarski's squad took over a hundred. That answer your question, Colonel?"

The colonel laughed. But his aide suddenly held up a hand. "Wait a second. SOS of some kind on the field telephone. Yes, yes . . . I get you. Yes. Ouvarski . . . a dozen men. What? Trapped in a barn . . . Okay. . . . But where, man, *where?*"

He saw the colonel reach out, and handed the phone to him.

The colonel consulted the map and noted the position of the barn. After a minute's delay, he got a battery commander by radio. Calmly, he gave the map location.

"Have that stone barn boxed in by your guns," he ordered. "Fire for five minutes exactly—and then quit. We'll have relief troops ready to move in then."

He handed the phone to Weller.

"I'm going down to the bridges now, Dobie," he said.

Captain Dobie looked white. "Ouvarski trapped," he repeated. "Can we spare enough men right now to get them out, sir?"

The aide said, "Why not?"

[*147*]

The colonel put a thin, dirty hand on Dobie's arm. "You *know* we'll get Ouvarski out. And my orders to you, sir, are to stay right here. You have my authority to make your man, Slim, a sergeant. Send him in command of the Ouvarski rescue bunch. Keep Weller with you. And *you*, Dobie, in future, try not to be so all-fired brave."

The captain turned to catch Weller's eye as the colonel marched across the road to his own hidden jeep.

"He sounds," Dobie said, "a good deal like me talking to André, doesn't he?"

But his smile was short.

"So Slim's a sergeant at last," he said. "Get him on the radio. Tell him to pick up fifteen or twenty men and we'll meet him down the road."

"But Captain," Weller exploded, "the colonel said—"

"Ouvarski's my lieutenant, and a brave one. It's *my* job to see that he and his men get out alive," Dobie snapped.

"Okay, sir," Weller said. "It's me'll get court-martialed. But pay no heed."

The jeep bounded and took to the road.

A few moments later they met Slim with a truckload of men, and instructed him to follow. They whirled past a château set on a hill, with a scattering of cottages on its lower slopes.

Weller tilted rapidly around high stone walls,

and pulled up in the shelter of a cottage near the château gates.

"Can't get any closer," Weller said firmly. "Ouvarski must be in that barn over there."

"We'll stay here till the shelling that the colonel ordered is over," Dobie ordered.

Slim had his men out of the truck and ready to move in.

Without warning, from unseen guns, a barrage of shells circled the barn. The men crouched near the jeep winced under the explosive pressure on their ears.

Captain Dobie had been watching his stopwatch. Five minutes later he said, "All right, Slim, shelling's over. Fan your men out, and take those Nazis in."

The new sergeant and his men moved rapidly ahead, skirting the cottage wall.

They had just disappeared around the corner when Dobie cried sharply, "What in the name of—"

Weller had sprung headlong from the jeep and lunged at a sunken doorway.

A moment later he returned, breathing hard, with a dog in his arms.

"*Patchou!*" Dobie shouted.

Weller, his face tilted away from Patchou's loving tongue and scrambling paws, pitched the dog into Captain Dobie's lap.

"If this means what I think it means," he puffed rapidly, "André's somewheres about. Maybe you can figure it out, sir. . . ."

Without waiting, he was gone, clanking with grenades, his head lowered between determined shoulders.

Straining forward in the jeep, Captain Dobie sat raging at his helplessness. He knew he would be useless in the field. He could barely walk. But every rifle crack, every grenade explosion sent his 'blood boiling. To think of André exposed to all this was a maddening extra anxiety.

He kept a hand on Patchou, who was torn between the joy of reunion with an old friend, and terror.

Dobie smoothed his fur absently while he directed his binoculars toward the heavy firing about the barn. He could not see much that was happening, because of the cottage wall, and stared around the fields. "If André'll only keep under cover till this shooting stops," Dobie thought.

He stiffened at the smell of timbers burning, and looked back to the barn quickly.

Slim appeared around the corner of the cottage and ran up toward Dobie.

"Cap'n," he panted. "More—" He stopped and stared wildly. "What's that dawg! That ain't—*It is* Patchou! Well, for cryin' out—"

"More what?" the captain snapped.

"More trouble, Cap'n. The barn's afire in one corner. An' we ain't got half the Germans yet. They're hid everywhere. If Ouvarski and the men have to make a break for it, there's still enough Nazis to pick 'em all off."

Dobie reached for the radio switch. Turning to Slim, he barked instructions.

"I'll order smoke shells to cover their escape. Go out there and warn the men to pull back a little. Where's Weller?"

Slim poised on one foot to answer.

"He's fightin' mad—an' he's fightin' good."

He disappeared into a thicket to carry out the captain's order. Dobie spoke rapidly into the radio and then signed off.

For a while he sat listening, and watching the smoke billow high above a gable of the barn.

He heard loud, sputtered German orders. Then came renewed rifle bursts, and a grenade exploded near by.

Just before the outburst, Patchou gave a high, excited yelp and leaped from the jeep.

"Patchou!" Captain Dobie shouted furiously. "Come here, boy. *Patchou!*"

The dog streaked, with flying tail, back toward the château gates, stretched to his utmost to cover ground.

With piercing yelps of delight he jumped into the arms of a girl. She had turned at his barking and then suddenly run to meet him.

Captain Dobie regarded the slim figure with amazement. Slacks, army jacket, man's cap from which soft black hair like André's escaped. And the same gray-blue eyes.

A flash of enlightenment burst over Dobie.

Irritated to fury, he muttered, "Jumping Jehosophat! Now we have *Marie* Gagnon!"

CHAPTER EIGHTEEN

The Secret Tunnel

CAPTAIN DOBIE'S heart and thoughts were with the men under his command. Beyond that, he was desperately aware of great armies fighting a hard battle near by.

Seeing Marie here, knowing André was also in the battle area, he thought angrily, "This is too much."

"Ma'moiselle," he shouted, "this is no place for you. Find cover immediately!"

Marie looked up. "You do not understand," she said. "This dog belongs to my brother. André must be here somewhere. Patchou couldn't get this far alone."

"I *do* know," replied the captain. "Get under that gateway quickly—and *hold* that dog."

When Marie crouched under the arch, he explained quickly how he had come to know André.

Marie said nervously, "You haven't seen him?"

"No! Since I left your home, I have not." The captain's voice was sharp with anxiety. "And I haven't time to look for him now. My men are in that burning barn with Germans all around it. I've ordered covering smoke shells dropped to help them escape. And I can't understand what's held the shells up."

He hesitated. Looking with deep concern at Marie, he spoke more gruffly. "I'm just afraid there's a good chance André may be in that barn."

Marie ran out a step or two and pointed.

"In *that* barn?" she cried. "Oh! I can get him out then. Come, Patchou!"

Captain Dobie stood up and shouted, but Marie and Patchou had disappeared through the cottage door—not across the field.

Captain Dobie sank back, fuming. The flames were spreading across the barn roof. He switched on the radio and waited irritably. When there was no response, he reached back into the jeep for grenades which he hooked into his belt.

He had just grasped his gun firmly, and gingerly lowered a leg to the ground, when Patchou barked and wriggled out of the cottage door.

At the same instant Slim came around the garden wall and stopped in his tracks, staring at the doorway.

"Ouvarski!" he shouted and then, "*André!*"

Captain Dobie's head snapped toward the cottage.

A tall officer stood behind Patchou, and with him was André.

Behind Lieutenant Ouvarski and André straggled several dusty, smoke-blackened men. They moved a few steps forward.

Ouvarski steadied himself against a stone pillar. Marie and two of the men eased a wounded soldier they were carrying, to the ground.

"Captain," Ouvarski said hoarsely, "can you get medics? Three wounded—one badly."

Captain Dobie swallowed hard. "Is that all?"

"All others accounted for, sir," Ouvarski reported. "No worse."

"Not any of you are accounted for," the captain growled. "How did you get *here?* I thought you were in that blasted barn."

Slim gasped as Marie, finished with making her patient more easy, walked forward.

Ouvarski simply threw out a hand toward Marie, and said, "She led us out."

Marie walked up to Captain Dobie.

"There's a tunnel to the barn from this gardener's cottage, sir," she explained. "I didn't have time to tell you before. The tunnel is old, but it is open. The Maquis have been using it for months, partly for wounded men. The barn was our headquarters. We just moved out yesterday."

Marie came up through the old tunnel

Captain Dobie nodded, speechless with relief. He pushed back his helmet, mopped his forehead, and switched on the radio. "I'll cancel those smoke shells," he muttered.

At that moment the air overhead whined ominously. A curtain of shells fell around the barn and exploded. A dense pall of white smoke drifted across the field.

"Where's Weller?" the captain asked Slim. "And what about the Nazis still around that barn?"

He was interrupted by grenade and rifle fire and the thrashing of men breaking through shrubbery.

"Watch it!" Weller's voice rang above the din.

The shooting stopped suddenly, and German and American voices mingled.

Captain Dobie listened a moment, smiled, and switched on the radio.

"Thanks for the smoke shells," he said into the receiver. He switched through to his command post. "Say, send along a couple of trucks for prisoners. And a medic and ambulance. At least three wounded here—one pretty bad."

He turned back to the others.

"Well, Ouvarski," he said pleasantly, "I certainly sent you into something. Headquarters said positively no Germans left in this area."

"They came out of this château and we had to take cover in the barn, sir," Ouvarski said.

"Take it easy," Dobie said, "all of you, till the trucks get here. Sergeant! What ails *you?*"

Weller limped into sight along the wall.

"We've about cleaned 'em all out—finally," he grinned.

Dobie frowned. "But what happened to you?"

"Got myself a bullet." Weller's smile broadened and turned into a grimace of pain.

"I thought I told you to stay away from those Germans," Dobie barked.

Weller limped painfully to the jeep and Slim spun him gently around and into the back seat.

"You sure did, sir," Weller said. "But you forgot to tell them Germans to keep away from me."

Not far behind Weller, a line of Nazi prisoners were coming across the field, hands on head. With them, on each side, strode Americans with Tommy guns ready.

Marie was examining the injury to Weller's leg. "That bullet will have to be taken out," she said. "It's not in very deep. It won't hurt much."

"It's gonna stay right there," Weller said. "It's probably the only proof I'll have to show my kids I was ever in this war."

André had been saying, "Sir," at intervals. But he had trouble saying it loud enough to make the captain hear.

When the prisoners had been herded together under guard a little distance away, Captain Dobie sank back in his seat and smiled down.

"André," he said, "I'm too glad to see you alive to tell you what I ought to."

André felt his face grow red. "I wanted to try to get my father and mother home."

"It would have been simpler for all of us if you had waited," replied the captain.

"I couldn't, sir," André said staunchly.

"If Patchou hadn't been here, Captain," Marie said, "I might have missed André. It was Patchou who found *me.*"

The dog, at the sound of his name, tossed up his head. Then he sniffed deeply, and whirled in the direction of the château gates, paused a brief second, and shot away at an excited gallop.

Captain Dobie could only say, *"Now* what?"

CHAPTER NINETEEN

The 82nd Finishes Its Fight

THE building which had housed the patients from the St. Sauveur hospital for a week was being emptied hastily.

A plump older nurse was helping the sick who could walk. Hurrying them into their wraps, she bustled them out to a line of waiting, ancient cars.

Doctors were aiding the more helpless patients.

All of them froze like statues when a shell crashed near by.

"Since dawn," scolded the nurse, "this racket has been going on. Now, one foot up into the car, dear. Now the other. That's my good girl. *Bon voyage.*"

The last to leave were the Gagnons. Pierre walked slowly toward the door with his arm around Mme. Gagnon. She moved stiffly, but without pain.

At the door a doctor smiled at them.

"Do not worry about madame, M. Gagnon," he said. "She is greatly improved. I expect no more difficulties for her."

"*Merci,* doctor," Pierre replied gruffly.

The doctor peered around the door. "I see that M. Angell is waiting for you in his car. I'm sure you will find his house a fortress of safety."

His words were drowned in the shriek and explosion of a second shell, and the rending crash of roof timbers. The blast hurtled the three of them into a corner. A shower of falling lath and plaster filled the room.

The doctor and Pierre pulled Mme. Gagnon to her feet.

From outside, the desperate voice of the car driver shrieked, "Hurry, doctor! Come at once! I do not intend to wait till another explosion hits my car."

Mme. Gagnon shook herself and with great dignity stated firmly, "I can walk. Observe your own step, Pierre. You, also, doctor."

She crossed the shattered porch and went down the steps. Pierre and the doctor raced to help her into the conveyance.

At the slam of the door, M. Angell was prepared, and the car leaped forward through the gates and into the lane.

Pierre gasped for breath. "I hope your home is safe," he said hoarsely.

"No place is safe today," the driver retorted over his shoulder, swinging the battered old car expertly around curves.

Braced as well as she could manage, Mme. Gagnon looked out with horror on the countryside.

"My son and my daughter!" she cried. "Could they exist through such warfare as this? I must know, Pierre. It is worse than I imagined."

The doctor spoke soothingly, but broke off to shout, "Angell. Watch yourself!"

A soldier had stepped out from the shelter of a ditch with upraised hand. "You must detour," he said in French. "This lane and the road beyond are mined." He pointed to one side. "Those fields are safe."

M. Angell muttered and nosed the car cautiously into the pasture. Circling shell holes, rocking over hummocks, he steered toward a shallow depression some distance ahead. After that he forced the car up a rise.

As they neared the top, the sound of machine guns and rifle fire, which had been muffled, seemed to explode all around them.

M. Angell brought the steaming car to a stop. He surveyed the landscape on all sides.

After a moment he said, "If you will be kind enough to alight, I shall lead you to safety—but on your own feet. We must abandon this vehicle to the mercies of Heaven."

Mme. Gagnon said to the doctor, "It is cause for rejoicing, doctor, that your cure was successful and I *can* walk. Stop frowning, Pierre. Each step I take leads toward home."

"At the moment," snapped M. Angell, "our steps lead down that slope on the left, toward those cottages. That path," and he pointed to the château, "leads to my house, but firing of considerable intensity is going on there."

A tremendous salvo of shells interrupted. Dense white smoke rolled over the hill and drifted through the trees lining the driveway to the château.

"It sounds as though we were moving directly into the middle of a battle," Mme. Gagnon said.

M. Angell raised his head. "There is a skirmish there on the other side of the hill, which I do not understand," he said.

Pierre Gagnon stared around.

At a fresh outbreak of gunfire Mme. Gagnon begged him to lower himself.

But Pierre's eyes were fixed wildly on a point near the cottages. His mouth dropped open and closed again excitedly.

"Maman!" he gasped. "Patchou! I see Patchou!"

The doctor and M. Angell turned to him in alarm.

Mme. Gagnon stood up. "I do not see Patchou," she cried. "But if he is here, certainly André must be near."

Suddenly the vague noises broke into a noisy scuffle on the rocky, brush-covered knoll above them. German and American voices rang out angrily.

"It is unbearable!" Mme. Gagnon cried. "I must find André!"

She broke and ran.

Pierre gave a lunge. He caught his wife's sleeve and was about to pull her to the ground when a racing dog, like a tornado, streaked up the slope.

Patchou danced to Pierre and then to Mme. Gagnon, lathering their hands in rapturous welcome, yelping shrilly.

An American soldier, his shoulders sagging with fatigue, came out of the underbrush. He frowned at the group. "What're you folks doing out here?" he demanded. "You better come along with me."

The doctor—the only one of the Normans who understood English—said, "Yes. Most certainly we do not wish to stay here."

The American started down the slope. Mme. Gagnon and Pierre, attended by the two other men, followed.

"But Pierre," Mme. Gagnon protested, "why do we follow them? Did Patchou come this way?"

Patchou answered this by tearing ahead with great purpose.

"You see," said Pierre.

At the foot of the slope the American pushed his way through a break in the hawthornes. At his heels, M. Angell and the doctor gallantly pulled the bushes apart for Mme. Gagnon.

She took a step forward and stood still, a hand clasped to her heart.

Not twenty feet away, standing near a jeep and a cluster of soldiers, were André and Marie.

At the same instant André and Marie saw her. And André hurled himself toward his mother.

"I knew I would find you!" he cried. "I *knew!*"

Marie and Pierre drew into the family embrace.

Slim and Weller turned to catch each other's eye. "The kid done it," Weller said.

Slim sighed. "I shore wish I had that trumpet now," he said. "I feel awful sentimental."

Captain Dobie sat back and smoked, watching the happy reunion of the Gagnon family.

When the doctor and M. Angell left to start up the hill Marie broke away from the family to run after them.

"Oh, Monsieur Angell," she called, "I must tell you how sorry I am your barn was burned. It was so useful to the Maquis. We are grateful to you for letting us use it."

"It is nothing," M. Angell replied courteously. "It was for France. However, if you will accept advice from a stranger, I suggest that you now return home with your mother."

Marie smiled. "I quite agree with you, M'sieur."

Within a few minutes, trucks and ambulances drew up. The wounded, both American and German, were cared for and taken away.

Weller and Captain Dobie resisted the suggestions of the medics to go back in the ambulance.

"We don't want no pamperin'," Weller said shortly. "I'm only nicked, anyway."

The fighting squads clambered aboard trucks to return to the St. Sauveur front.

The captain leaned from the jeep to talk more easily with Mme. Gagnon and Pierre.

The radio in the car squawked insistently.

"Answer that signal, will you, Weller?" Captain Dobie said.

Weller snapped a switch, said, "Okay, Colonel," and gave his report on Ouvarski's rescue.

Then he listened a few minutes and exclaimed, "Yes, Colonel . . . I'll tell the cap'n. Sure will."

Captain Dobie had stopped talking to listen to Weller.

André asked curiously, "Good news?"

Weller almost shouted, "Our armies are cleanin' up St. Sauveur, and the 47th're movin' on past— headin' for the coast an' then Cherbourg."

"Good," said Dobie. "Is that all?"

"Nope." Weller grinned. "The colonel says the 82nd won't be goin' on to Cherbourg with the 9th Division. We're ordered to take the marshy country south of St. Sauveur. *An' after that we'll get relieved.*"

"The 82nd will be out of the war?" Dobie asked.

"Every bloomin' man of us," Weller replied. "An' that means you, too, Cap'n."

Slim winked at André. "I guess that means you, too, kid," he said.

Captain Dobie rubbed his hand across his eyes, and said, "After over two weeks of steady fighting I guess the 82nd deserves a rest. Well, give me that phone, Weller."

When he had finished his call he said to Pierre, "I have sent for a jeep to take you home, M. Gagnon. Do you think you can hang onto André till the jeep gets here?"

Pierre threw back his head in his great, bellowing laugh. "I think so, *mon Capitaine*," he roared.

"Never mind, kid," Weller said. "I promise you we'll be back. We'll see you in a week'r two. You just save us some of that good fresh milk."

Pierre clapped his hand to his head and glared at André.

"*Mon Dieu!*" he shouted. "The cows!"

CHAPTER TWENTY

Bastille Day—1944

THAT night, lights glowed in the Gagnon house. In spite of the blustery cold wind and drifts of rain, the door stood open most of the evening.

Friends came, laughing, crying, chattering greetings and news. Children came to ask André questions and stand with open mouths at what he had to say.

Marie brought cups of hot chocolate and black bread. Mme. Lescot supplied some small cakes.

Leon Duplis rode over to tell Marie that General de Gaulle, who commanded the Maquis from London, was now touring the liberated towns of Normandy.

"The French Army will soon join the fight to free our country," Leon whispered to Marie. "They will enter France from the Mediterranean.

But do not tell anyone yet I said so." And with that he was on his motor bike and gone.

On the road outside, traffic was coming up from the beach, but in smaller convoys. "The sea is getting very rough," someone reported.

By midnight all the guests had gone and the whole family were in bed—really home at last.

André went out to the road many times the next few days to look for friends on the army trucks and jeeps rolling by. On the third day, a messenger from St. Sauveur, on his way to the supply dumps on the beach, stopped to talk.

"We got the peninsula cut off now," he reported. "The 9th Division an' the 79th an' the 4th Division are on their way to Cherbourg. Goin' fast, too."

Captain Dobie's men were still fighting for the marshes and some hills west and south of St. Sauveur, he said.

The storm over the Channel had built up to an alarming degree. Rain and wind whipped the trees along the coast and drove the villagers indoors. Traffic past the house slowed almost to a stop.

When André asked a truck driver what was happening on the beaches, the driver said, "A blasted hurricane. The sea is standin' on end. No landin' barges can get ashore. Pretty bad, 'cause General Bradley's howlin' for ammunition."

Frenchmen coming to the village from the shore said tons of supplies had been swept away and sunk.

The storm raged for four days, and André went sadly about his duties watching the road now nearly empty of trucks.

Two days after the storm subsided, André heard that General Eisenhower had ferried across the Channel to look over the destruction.

"He'll talk to them army engineers an' get deliveries speeded up—or else," a soldier said.

But the Americans were driving hard to capture Cherbourg. They needed the port more than ever since the storm had stopped supplies coming across the beaches.

On June 28th, Leon came, and shouted through the door, "André! Marie! *Cherbourg has fallen. Normandy belongs to us again!*"

Then, on D-day plus 29—four weeks after the 82nd paratroopers had first drifted down into the Gagnon orchard—Slim clattered up in a jeep.

André saw him from the hallway and raced out to grab his hand and pump it up and down—as the soldiers did. He asked, "Where are Captain Dobie and Sergeant Weller? Has the 82nd been relieved? Did you win your battle?"

"What you mean, mister?" Slim growled. "Did we win our battle? The 82nd always wins its battles—Africa, Sicily, Normandy. You know that."

André took Slim into the house to see the rest of the family. He translated Slim's "American" as well as he could for his father and mother.

"This is my last errand this way," Slim told them. "I'm on my way to the Utah airstrip to fix the cap'n's passage home."

Before he left, he promised to bring Weller and the captain to see them on the way to the plane.

The storm had at last blown itself out, and traffic on the road was again heavy. Now the Allies were getting ready to break through to Paris—to free the rest of France. The British and Canadians were fighting hard around Caen. The Germans were bringing up more and more tanks—better in some ways than the British and American ones— and the battle was rough. But the Invasion armies were moving toward the breakout into the farther parts of France. The spirit of Liberty swept slowly but excitedly across all Normandy.

July 14th, Bastille Day, which was the symbol of French Liberty, would soon be here.   ..

"This year we will celebrate Bastille Day with good heart," said M. Blanc to Father Duprey.

And Father Duprey, who was very practical, asked, "How?"

"Ah, that I have thought about," M. Blanc answered. "And I have a plan for our little village. Alone, we cannot do justice to such a great event as this Liberation. We will join with Ste. Mère

Église to celebrate. We are not without talent in this village." He looked mysterious and whispered his plans to the priest, so that no one could overhear.

When they had finished their discussion, Father Duprey said, "Your plan will also keep the children out of the fields till the German land mines have been cleared up."

The following few days there was a great hubbub in the loft of the Gagnon barn. Children's voices rang out. And music billowed over the rooftops.

Early one morning, Father Duprey summoned André. Victor appeared with his cart, and with the priest and André jogged off, behaving mysteriously, to talk to the mayor of Ste. Mère Église.

Bastille Day, Friday, July 14th, was the next day. By sunrise that morning all the little villages near Ste. Mère were alive with activity.

Mothers bustled breakfast into their families and packed up lunch baskets. Older sisters swept the family's best clothes, all nicely aired, over the heads of the younger children. Then mothers and big sisters pulled and twisted themselves into their own gayest Normandy dresses. Fathers put on the dark suits they had been married in.

And all over the peninsula the French tricolor flags, which had been hidden away, flew in great flapping bursts of triumph from every house.

All churchbells that had survived the bombing began to ring soon after the sun was up.

In the Gagnon house, Maman was scurrying about, her own silk dress rustling as excitedly as she was. Marie, too, rustled in her new pale-yellow parachute gown.

Old cars had been rolled out of sheds where they had been hidden, and somehow brought to life. They began to ease into the busy military traffic and headed for Ste. Mère. Carts, bright with flags and flowers, and loaded with chattering villagers, thronged the roads.

Father Duprey and M. Blanc had gone to Ste. Mère still earlier in a borrowed car.

In good time, Victor, Mme. Lescot, and their daughter showed up at the Gagnon door with La Fumée. The fat Percheron whinnied when André led the family out to jam themselves into the cart.

When La Fumée entered the outskirts of Ste. Mère the town was already aflame with a noisy celebration.

Victor found a spot where La Fumée could be hitched to a post with a pail of water beside her.

In the heart of Ste. Mère Église the square was a churning mass of people. But in a cleared space in the center of the green, officials and police were arranging things in an orderly way. There was a flag-draped table on a raised platform, and rows of chairs for special personages stood in a square.

At one side of the table, dignitaries were gathering. At the other side, M. Blanc and the Ste. Mère music master were herding the children who were to sing, into neat rows.

Running to join the children, André saw uniformed French officers in a group among the dignitaries. All eyes were upon them. Farther back stood a company of about a hundred American soldiers.

Marie went to join Leon, Jacquard, and the other Maquis who had been able to come.

When the hour for opening the ceremonies arrived, Father Duprey and two other priests moved to the table for prayers of thanksgiving.

Then the mayor of Ste. Mère, and the mayors of other villages made speeches. These over, the music master blew his pitch pipe and M. Blanc raised his arm to give the beat for the singing. High and clear, the children's voices sang out the beloved old songs of triumphant France.

When the last song died away the children settled down on the grass, and M. Blanc rose.

"We are now about to have a special pleasure," he announced. "André Gagnon will express the feeling of comradeship we all have for our friends, the Americans."

André had been carefully carrying his trumpet under his arm. His knees shaking, he stepped forward and put the trumpet to his lips.

He played first a gay little Normandy tune. This was loudly applauded and he waited for the noise to die down.

When he again trilled out a trumpet call, every Frenchman present grew silent and listened with puzzled eyes. The tune was one they didn't know.

Suddenly, from the back of the crowd, men's voices began to sing the words.

André's heart gave a great leap. But he kept on playing. The voices were growing louder. The men were moving toward the green.

André swept into the chorus, and powerfully the American words, punctuated by clapping

hands at the proper time, swelled out over the crowd.

A French voice took up the words. Another and another, until the entire gathering was singing.

Many of the Americans stood beside André now, and Slim, his hard hands beating the clap-clap of the chorus, sang the loudest.

"Deep in ze 'eart ohff Tayxsas," sang the French.

"Stars at night are big and bright,
 (clap-clap, clap-clap,) *Deep in the heart of Texas,*

Remind me of the one I love,
 (clap-clap, clap-clap) *Deep in the heart of Texas,"*

sang Slim and Weller and Captain Dobie, dragging out the last long notes at the thought of home.

André dropped his trumpet to his side.

As the babble of happy voices rose and became bedlam, Captain Dobie shook hands with the French officers.

André started at the sight of a Royal Air Force uniform and ran across the square.

Standing beside Marie, Ronald Pitt was laughing with the Maquis over the escapade of the strange "nun."

Ronald grabbed André's arms and swung him merrily around.

"How did *you* get here, Ronald?" André asked.

"Well," Ronald replied, "I'm on my way to the British lines to chauffeur a general around—"

"Oh-ohh," André giggled.

"I saw this celebration going on down here," Ronald Pitt went on, "and I wanted to see what was happening in Ste. Mère. So I landed in a field and trotted over—and look what I found!"

Slim and Weller joined them then.

"Didn't we tell you we'd come?" demanded Weller.

Softly, a song began to tremble from different points among the crowd.

André lifted his trumpet and began to play.

And swelling mightily over the battered roofs of Ste. Mère rolled out the song of freedom that is the voice of France—the "Marseillaise."

Everyone sang and many wept.

After that, the gathering broke up and lunch baskets were opened. Mme. Gagnon beckoned her enlarged family party together under the shade of a wide chestnut tree. Lunch was spread out. Between them, she and Mme. Lescot had brought food enough for all.

Captain Dobie and André sat side by side.

"You will return to visit us after the war?" André asked shyly.

"I certainly will," promised the captain. "I shall come back whenever I can. I won't be comfortable unless I know what you're up to."

André laughed. "And," he said, "I shall go to America some day to see that you have got that leg mended."

"*Vive les Americains!*" shouted Raoul, who had mysteriously become one of the group.

"*Vive la French!*" shouted Weller.

La Fumée heard them, and put her muzzle down comfortably into the water pail.

About the Author

CLAYTON KNIGHT was born in Rochester, New York, and grew up just in time to become an airplane pilot with the famed Lafayette Escadrille in World War I. He also had a box seat for World War II in which he served in every important theater of war as an Associated Press special correspondent. His lifelong, active interest in aviation has earned him many honors and taken him to almost every corner of the earth, most recently on a round-the-world trip collecting material for an official history of the Military Air Transport Service. It has also provided him with fascinating material for a distinguished list of books and magazine stories that have made him well known both to young people and adults, not only as an author but an artist of uncommon distinction.

About the Historical Consultant

Few experts are as well qualified as MAJOR GENERAL RALPH ROYCE to pass on the merits of a book about the Normandy invasion. As Deputy Commander of the Ninth Air Force, he was the senior air officer afloat during the invasion of France and served aboard the cruiser *Augusta* with Admiral Kirk and General Bradley. He accompanied General Bradley to shore at Utah Beach and, in the days that followed, reconnoitered the surrounding country very thoroughly, visiting many of the towns mentioned in this book. In General Royce's words, "Mr. Knight's book brings back very vividly the life that we lived during those hectic and exciting days in June, 1944, and portrays extremely well the life of the countryside during those early hours of the invasion that led to the freeing of France from the yoke of the invader."

WE WERE THERE BOOKS

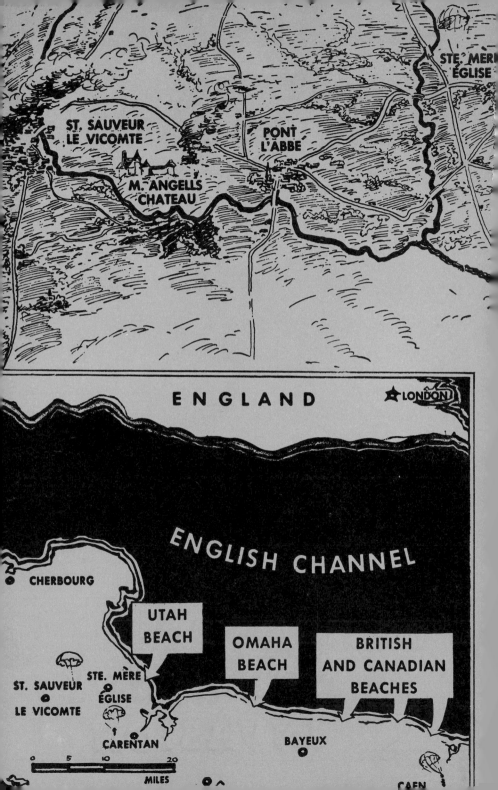